D1248136

THE SLEEPER

by

HOLLY ROTH

AN INNER SANCTUM MYSTERY
PUBLISHED BY
SIMON AND SCHUSTER
NEW YORK

PUBLISHED BY SIMON AND SCHUSTER, INC.
ROCKEFELLER CENTER, 630 FIFTH AVENUE
NEW YORK 20, N. Y.

MANUFACTURED IN THE UNITED STATES OF AMERICA

For

JULIAN MULLER

With my love and gratitude

THE SLEEPER

I

He had made and finished his breakfast and was standing forlornly in the hall surveying the insane chaos—the apartment had been wrecked, and the ruins then tossed about in an orgy of apparently insane vandalism—when the doorbell rang.

He hoped it would be the maid, Lena, who always rang with cautious but wasted tact before she used her key, and so the two men standing on the threshold were a disappointment. He said, "Yes?"

"Mr. Robert Kendall?"

"Yes."

"May we speak with you for a moment?"

"Why, yes." Kendall stepped back a half step, and then reconsidered. "No. That is—"

He didn't see how he could word it without sounding either foolish or childishly frightened, so he didn't try, but put it flatly: "You will have to identify yourselves before I can ask you in." If they were Fuller Brush salesmen or charity organizers or telephone repairmen, they would be mightily surprised, he thought.

But they didn't look as if they fell into any of those categories, and they showed a total lack of surprise. The taller, slenderer of the two, a carroty-headed, youthful-looking man of thirty-two or three, said, "Of course. I am

Eric Gregory, FBI. This"—he gestured at his companion, a sedate-looking, executive type of about forty—"is Major Windham of the CIC." The major was wearing a rather tight blue suit with a faint pin stripe.

Kendall said, "I see." But he didn't move. Their arrival seemed too fortuitous.

Gregory, as if he understood Kendall's hesitation, withdrew a leather case from his pocket and held it out for Kendall's inspection. Windham hesitated and then followed suit. In the redhead's case, the motion had the air of a routine gesture, but Major Windham's was a slow and grudging action. He apparently resented the necessity of identifying himself.

But the credentials were very impressive. Kendall abruptly felt foolish. He pushed the door wider and said, "Come in." And, as he threaded his way ahead of them through the littered hall, he offered a little apology in the form of "Coffee?"

Windham said, "No, thank you." He had a very deep voice, and he somehow managed to inject pomposity into the three words.

In the living room Kendall picked two seat cushions off the floor and fitted them into the two chairs in which they belonged, noticing, as he did so, that one of them had been slashed so that the stuffing was escaping. He felt a return of anger as he waved the two men to the chairs and sat himself down on the couch. That anger, and his growing inward confusion of the past few weeks suddenly, and not very logically, centered itself in the two men before him.

He asked, "Is this call merely a coincidence, or had you learned of my—visitors?"

There was a little pause. Then Gregory said, "The police advised us of the attempted robbery."

"Really?" Sergeant Vincent of the New York City police force hadn't seemed to Kendall bright enough or interested enough to make the connection.

Gregory tilted his head in confirmation, and then asked in a bland voice, "Are you surprised, Mr. Kendall?"

Oh, no, you don't, Kendall thought. He hadn't done a damn thing, and they weren't going to succeed in their neat little trick of getting him on the defensive, full of disclamatory explanations. He used what he always thought of as "the feminine form"—answering a question with a question: "Should I be?"

The conversation, if it could be called that, died. And that's another trick of the trade, Kendall decided. Most people can't bear a vacuum. Well, I can. He tightened the belt of his robe as if it were his self-possession, and sank comfortably back against the couch's pillows.

Gregory didn't let the pause lengthen, and as he resorted to a straightforward question, Kendall felt a small throb of victory. Gregory asked, "Why didn't you get in touch with us, Mr. Kendall?"

"You mean when I found the house ransacked like this?"

Before Gregory could answer, Windham thrust his chin forward and boomed, "Or whenever it started. What was it that happened before the ransacking?"

They *were* shrewd, Kendall conceded. And he wasn't

so smart as he thought he was. His question did imply that the housebreaking was not the first incident, but Major Windham had been extraordinarily quick in spotting the implication.

Kendall said slowly, "To answer both questions—I didn't get in touch with you because it simply never occurred to me. It all started yesterday afternoon with two phony attempts to get hold of the manuscript. Why should I have reported that to you?—'CIC' stands for 'Counter Intelligence Corps,' doesn't it, Major?"

The major nodded pontifically. There was something about him that irritated Kendall. He had the look of solidity that bankers often cultivate; for one thing, he wasn't over forty years old, but he looked indefinably older. It was as if, Kendall thought, he was reaching for seniority, eldership. His bearing was erect, but not military—rather it was pompous. By leaning slightly backward, he created the effect of a stomach. Kendall decided, rather baselessly, that Windham's belly was probably as flat as a board.

Windham repeated, "'CIC' is an abbreviation for Counter Intelligence Corps."

Now, why hadn't he simply said yes? Kendall felt he was being childish, but nevertheless his irritation was growing. He asked, "And it's a division of the Army?"

Windham inclined his head majestically.

"Then why should I have notified *you?* The Army okayed publication of the articles. You were willing to have the whole world see them, so why on earth should I expect you to be interested in the fact—possibility—that someone is trying to get a glimpse ahead of the rest?"

Gregory spoke up in a conciliatory voice—he had a pleasant voice, and a pleasant, boyish face—"Just *because* it was so pointless, Mr. Kendall. Look—why don't you tell us all about it?"

"Well, certainly. If you think it necessary." Kendall made an effort to overcome his feeling of antagonism, and as a result his voice sounded flat, almost purposefully uninteresting. "As I told you, the first incident occurred yesterday afternoon. It was about four o'clock. I had just come home from downtown. . . ."

II

It was about four o'clock, and Kendall had just returned from downtown. When the doorbell rang, he was leaning against the frame of his living room archway, his hands in his overcoat pockets, feeling dispirited. The room didn't look clean—it *wasn't* clean. Opposite him, sleet beat against the windows, and the dull roar of Manhattan traffic formed a dreary obbligato to the sleet's slushy beat. As he stood gazing unseeingly across the untidy room he had a desire to go somewhere, anywhere. Maybe I'll take a trip, he thought. It isn't that I mind the weather. And I don't mind living alone. But the domestic part of it defeats me. No matter what I do— The doorbell rang.

He turned his head so that he was looking down the short hall at the front door of his apartment, but he made no move toward it. The bell represented another of his domestic problems. He did not want trial boxes of soap suds; he did not want to contribute to strange, never-before-heard-of charities; and he had come to dislike without discrimination all the blithe young men and women researchers who seemed to be collecting data on every facet of human life as lived in New York City in the twentieth century.

The bell rang again. He moved slowly down the hall and opened the door.

In the outer hallway stood a small man wearing a soggy, visored cap. He looked at Kendall's feet and said in a rusty, disinterested singsong, "Pickup for the *Courier*."

"What pickup?" Kendall asked.

The man looked up at him with vague irritation on his dirty face. "*I* don't know. Here"—he brought a small pink scrap of paper up to his nose and slowly deciphered—"'Pick up carbon of manuscript, Apartment 4C, Robert Kendall.' That you?"

"Yes, but they know I don't have a carbon; we've been through all that. Are you from the *Courier*?" Before the man replied, Kendall knew the answer. Nothing associated with the dignified *Courier* could be as unkempt as this bedraggled messenger.

The man said cryptically, "Quick and speedy service."

"What? Oh." Kendall translated it mentally with capitals— Quick & Speedy Service. An outside messenger service. "Well, if you'll wait a minute I'll call the *Courier* and—"

The messenger said, "Naw," and moved to the elevator.

There was a slap of insolence in the syllable, and a small spring inside of Kendall tightened for a second. But the second passed and the spring unwound, as it usually did with him. That was one of the reasons the doorbell created such havoc in his life—he was almost incapable of rudeness and, as a result, he permitted the stream of bell pushers to absorb a disproportionate amount of his time.

He closed the door quietly and went back through his inner hall to the front of the apartment. This time he bypassed the living room and went into the small bedroom on his left. It was after four o'clock, but the bed hadn't been made. He had left the apartment at ten that morning; Lena, the twice-a-week maid, had been due at eleven.

Well—he shrugged, threw his overcoat on a chair, and tackled the bed—obviously she had had another "bad" day.

He was in the middle of the task when the phone rang. The room was too small for him to move around in with comfort, and as he circled the bed to get to the telephone he tripped over the trailing blankets and crashed against the wall. His own heft made it a jarring collision. By the time he had disentangled himself and picked up the phone his formless irritation of the past half-hour had culminated in an unusual but intense fury.

His "hello" was a bark.

The man on the other end of the wire said, "Mr. Kendall?"

"Yes!"

"Oh." The voice proceeded with more caution, as if tiptoeing. "My name is Johnson—Fred Johnson. I'm in the promotion department of Salway & Gibbons. They tell me in editorial that they don't have a script of your book, *Genesis of Treason*—?" He sounded delicately incredulous and gently outraged.

Kendall took a deep breath. He said, "The book's not scheduled until fall."

"Well, yes, but the thing *is* that we have production schedules *far* in advance. For promotion, you know. Copy has to be written, suitable plates made, book has to be assigned—"

Kendall said tensely, "Now, look—I've been through all that with Lou Salway. Take it up with him."

"Well, all right, but if you happen to have a script on *hand*—"

Kendall never heard the end of the sentence. He hung up.

He sat still on the edge of the bed and forced himself to calmness. What was the matter with him? Was he so poorly balanced that an irritation as small as the defection of Lena could start a spiral of bad temper that reached a point where he slammed telephone receivers down on people who were simply trying to do their jobs?

He had never had a greater right to be happy—or, at the least—content. All he had ever really asked of life, almost more than he had dared ask, was about to come to pass with the publication of *Genesis of Treason,* and with its current serialization in the *Weekly Courier*. A few months before, the possibility of his by-line's appearing in the pages of that most honored of the nation's weekly magazines had been remote to the point of fantasy. So why this tension, this clenched-fist frenzy— He carefully unknotted his big hands and then stared down at them as, pressure released, the red poured back into the palms.

But he knew why; he really knew what was upsetting him. He had not admitted it to himself, but he was subconsciously aware that since the suicide of Buddy Hollister a month before he had been in a mounting state of tension. But, he told himself firmly, that was ridiculous. Hollister had been nothing to him—just a crazy kid, a charming young man, a blond, curly-headed psychopath, a slender, graceful prisoner poised against a background of steel bars, a pensive spinner of anecdotes, a laughing fabulist— A cold-blooded traitor? A fascist? A Communist? An enigma.

And *that,* Kendall decided with a mental swoop after the elusive explanation, that amorphousness, that chimerical quality in Hollister was what was haunting him.

Kendall had known others who had died. Certainly. He had known suicides, too. His father had committed suicide when his mother walked out. Kendall was seventeen then —old enough to understand most of the implications and all of the blatant facts, and he had sympathized deeply with his father, as, indeed, he had all his life sided with his father in the deadly war that raged unceasingly between his quiet, dependable father and his unstable, cheating mother.

And there had been that corporal in Luzon who killed himself the night before a scheduled attack; then the attack had not taken place. The irony, the bitter waste, had engraved the incident in Kendall's memory. And he had known that corporal better than he had known Hollister.

. . . "He had known the corporal better . . ." Well, he hadn't known Buddy Hollister at all. Kendall had written a book, a detailed analysis of Francis Burton Hollister, First Lieutenant, United States Army, traitor, sentenced to thirty years' imprisonment by a military court for an act of espionage, presumed to be a Communist (although no statement to that effect had ever been overtly reported in the newspapers, because they were never told the exact nature of Hollister's crime). He had written a definitive treatise on Hollister, and he didn't know a thing about the boy, and now he never would.

Well. He stood up. He had been exposed to puzzles before. The world was full of puzzles. It was foolish, and usually profitless, to brood over them.

But he didn't complete his motion toward the tangled blankets. Instead, almost without volition, he went back to the side of the bed and, standing, dialed Salway & Gibbons' number. The major puzzles were giant clouds that, once admitted, obscured your thinking processes, but the little puzzles were wisps of smoke that merely irritated, and it was better, whenever possible, to blow them away.

He said into the phone, "Mr. Louis Salway, please." And again: "Mr. Louis Salway. Robert Kendall calling."

"Hello, Lou? Kendall.

". . . Fine. No, nothing new. Just wanted to ask you: Do you have a Fred Johnson in your promotion department?

". . . No? No, not John Littman—Fred Johnson.

". . . No, huh? Any Johnson in the whole joint?

". . . Got any guys there with ladylike voices? . . . Well, guess I have my people mixed."

He listened to Salway, a voluble man, for a while, said no, thanks, to a cocktail party, and agreed to call him in a few days.

After he had hung up Kendall sat down in a straight chair and absently contemplated the unmade bed. Then he reached down to the lower shelf of the bedside table and brought up the Manhattan telephone directory.

There was no Quick & Speedy Service listed.

He closed the book and held it in his lap.

So the smoky wisp hadn't been blown away. The little puzzle just led to the bigger one.

Apparently someone was trying to get a look at a complete manuscript of *Genesis of Treason*. Now, why would anyone go to that trouble? The story was running serially in the *Weekly Courier*, and the publication date had been pushed forward so that the first installment was already on the newsstands. In less than six weeks the whole article would be available to anyone who had a little patience and a little over a dollar in cash.

It would be nice to think that his style was irresistible—Kendall grimaced wryly—but it wasn't a very convincing or likely assumption. Still, for *some* reason *someone* didn't want to wait.

In a way, Kendall thought, it was as if Hollister wasn't quite dead. The enigma of him was still alive, the questions that surrounded him hadn't been killed off. The would-be thief who was trying to get the manuscript was not very different from the public as a whole. They, too, were still asking questions. They apparently didn't consider Hollister's suicide a confession of guilt. On the contrary, they seemed to feel that it had been motivated by the despair of innocence, that the boy had been hounded to death.

The American public never have liked courts-martial, he thought; it goes against everything they're brought up to believe.

And this one in particular had been so closed-door, so hush-hush, so big-brass.

Hollister's photographs hadn't done anything to quell the public's uneasiness in the face of a possible miscarriage of justice. The big brass hadn't been able to stop the press from running old shots of Hollister—Hollister laughing into the sun; Hollister looking determined in a football helmet; Hollister, young, pensive, manly, in a studio graduation pose. The traditional picture of the American Boy—handsome but not pretty, stalwart but not beefy, good but not goody-goody.

The public had questions, and they weren't going to be happy until they were answered. Now, having been whipped up by some dignified advance publicity on the part of the *Courier's* promotion department, they were looking forward to Kendall's series in the hope that it would provide the answers to some of those questions.

But Kendall had questions, too, and it looked as if he weren't going to be permitted to forget them.

III

He tried, in the flat voice, to show no sign of confusion, of unanswered questions. He told Gregory and Windham about the events in as few words as possible: a messenger had come, purporting to be from the magazine, asking for a carbon. Then someone had telephoned, said they were from his publishers. He had checked back. No such messenger service, no such person at the publishing house.

"I see." Gregory remained pleasant and bland, but traces of dissatisfaction showed on his youthful face. "And that's all?"

"That's all."

"I see." Gregory looked down absent-mindedly at the coffee table. The marble top had been pried out of its wrought-iron base, to expose the dusty shallow gap between stand and top. He said, almost aimlessly, as if he were seeking a starting point, "Did you doubt the messenger's legitimacy of purpose from the moment you saw him?"

"Why, no. I didn't give him another thought until the second incident—the telephone call."

Windham had an irritating habit of thrusting out his chin before he snapped up a point. Now his lower jaw pushed forward and he said, "Well, if you thought the messenger was from the *Courier* then why didn't you give him a carbon?"

Kendall said calmly, "Because I don't have one. I'm my own typist. I was negligent in the first place in making only a couple of carbons, and then I used them in marking up revises. When I retyped the final version, the carbons were no good—chewed to pieces. I threw them away. And after the messenger and the telephone call gave me reason to think about it, I realized that the *Courier* knew very well that I didn't have a carbon. They had asked me for one so they could do some routine styling while the original was still being held up by the Army. And Salway & Gibbons had read the final version after the Army okayed it, and then they had agreed to wait for galleys."

Windham said obstinately, "And that's all?"

The reiterated phrase grated on Kendall's nerves, and he showed open irritation for the first time. "What do you mean, 'That's all'? That's all there is about galleys. That's all that happened until I returned home last night and found this." He waved a hand at the tangled and dismembered mass of furniture.

Windham's jaw was very prominent. "Returned from where?"

There was a small silence in the room. Kendall had spent over three and a half war years in the Army, where he had acquired the rank of buck sergeant. He had also acquired the standard GI reaction to officers.

He said very slowly, with careful impersonality, "I think you are confused, Major. The military is not running this country. If you feel that these events—the attempts to get a manuscript, the rifling of my apartment—are of interest to you and the Army I'm glad to coöperate by—" He stopped, and then added deliberately, "by permitting you to come in, sit down, and talk to me. But you are far off base if you think I have to account to you for my movements."

He watched with a pleasant feeling of emancipation as Windham's pouter-pigeon front quivered in the face of an insubordination he could do nothing to quell.

Gregory seemed to have a ready supply of oil for troubled waters, but underlying his polite placidity there was an element of sternness. "You misunderstand, Mr. Kendall. Major Windham is upset by these events, seriously upset, and so his manner—and so he may not be completely tactful. He does not mean to imply that you would—and I am sure you do not intend to, uh, obstruct us. Perhaps the fact that you saw Miss Wentwirth last night has simply slipped your mind?"

Kendall's head jerked in Gregory's direction. His sense of outrage was almost obscured by his astonishment. "Have you been *following* me?" he demanded.

Gregory said, "No, no—" And Windham said, "We have kept careful track of the Wentwirth girl."

"Oh." Kendall absorbed the idea slowly. They had been following the Wentwirth girl all those weeks. And so of course they knew that he had seen her.

He said coldly, "Let's get this straight. You asked me what happened and I told you what happened. The things that happened *to* me, not the things I initiated. I saw Miss

Wentwirth because I wished to. I am unable to consider my talk with her as one of a series of events that might be of interest to you."

Windham said, "She is part of the Hollister case."

It was the first time the name had been spoken in the room.

Kendall said, appreciating the foolishness of the statement even as he made it, "I thought the Hollister case was closed."

And Gregory said softly, "Does it look it?" He pointed at the dismantled coffee table.

There was no answer to that.

Kendall pulled on the braided cord around his waist. "What do you *want* of me?" he asked stiffly. "I saw the Wentwirth girl. That's all there was to that. Not a new fact emerged as a result of our conversation. It didn't occur to me to mention the meeting, because I sincerely didn't think it was any of your business. I–"

Windham said, "One minute, Mr. Kendall. Please–just a minute." He leaned forward and put his elbows on his knees. Kendall had a sudden, inexplicable, but intense curiosity about the man. A vivid vision of Windham at home arose before him–Windham in a smoking jacket, but not smoking, sitting under a pool of light, in a deep, old-fashioned armchair. The light was coming over his left shoulder from a bridge lamp. A book was lying in his lap, and every one of the sparse hairs on his head was in perfect order. Across the room sat a meek-looking woman with a sewing basket in her lap. Her pool of light, thrown from a table lamp at her elbow, was not so strong as Windham's, her chair not so comfortable.

Windham cleared his throat, recalling Kendall to his own living room. Windham's face, suspended over his knees, looked very earnest. He said, "You see, Mr. Kendall—" He paused and cleared his throat again, and Kendall realized with a little feeling of shock that Windham was trying to unbend. He thought with a kind of impatient despair, Me, and my ridiculous attempts at figuring people out. It's just not as simple as all that. You can't peg them. Maybe he keeps a bleached mistress who gets drunk every night and makes his life an incessant hell. Maybe the outside of him is a defense against the inside. Maybe—

Windham said, "It's difficult to explain our interest without encroaching—without stepping into areas you consider your personal business. We are inclined to think the girl is very, very slick. The first of your series in the *Courier* would lead one to believe that you felt the same way. We just wouldn't want you, uh, to be taken in—"

Taken in . . .

IV

After his discovery that there was no Quick & Speedy Service in the telephone book, Kendall had sat on the straight chair in his bedroom, contemplated the unmade bed, thought of Hollister, thought of the pictures of him that had appeared in the papers, thought of the girl.

The mercurial Hollister had made him feel unusually heavy and slow. Had he been slow? Had Hollister taken him in? The girl—

The memory of the girl, he realized, was at the very heart of his gnawing indecision, of his inability to consider the story finished and dismiss it, of his bad temper, and of his desire to flee the city, the country, the continent.

Somebody had lied. Hollister—or the girl. All logic said it was the girl, but Kendall had never been satisfied with that logic. And the whole thing hadn't died with Hollister, wasn't over with the writing of the story, because now someone was mixing in, trying to get the manuscript, trying to trick him into—what?

He opened the heavy telephone directory that still lay on his knees and looked up Wentwirth, Marta. Then he dialed the number.

He said, "Miss Wentwirth?"

"Yes."

"This is Bob Kendall."

There was silence at the other end.

"Perhaps you don't remember me," he added diffidently. "I came to see you a couple of months ago—"

"Mr. Kendall, you certainly can't think I've forgotten you. Or your name. The *Courier* is lying in front of me right this minute. Your name—in red—is on the cover. *My* name is plastered all over the inside. You call me a liar—"

"No, Miss Wentwirth. Please—just a minute. I didn't. By *not* reporting your version—"

"All right. You call me a traitor—"

"No, I—"

"—a consort of traitors. You suggest—"

"Miss Wentwirth—"

"Let's put it this way: I didn't go to work yesterday or today. I doubt that I'll ever go into that office again. I've worked there for almost four years, and I've worked myself up— And *why* did you ruin it for me? For what? What did I *do?*" Her voice rose and broke.

He said into his horrified silence, "May I buy you a drink?"

"*What?*"

The shocked incredulity in her voice brought him up short. It was, he realized, utterly natural. She thought of him as—he corrected the phrase with stubborn honesty—he *was* her enemy, had treated her as an enemy. But that wasn't exactly how he had intended it.

He went doggedly on, knowing the effort wasted:

"There is an explanation. There may even be a way to—to extricate you. Let me come around and talk to you."

She said, and she sounded very tired, "All right."

The easy capitulation left him momentarily wordless with surprise. He had set himself for a long, and probably hopeless, struggle. He collected himself and said, "Good. Then I'll come right over. Okay?"

"Yes." She hung up.

He got his overcoat out of the closet, glanced absently at the still unmade bed, and walked down his hall. As he took his hat off the table, he looked back at the hall. Not very neat, no. But—pleasant. He liked the thought of "home." The concept. Another thought came, unrelated, unbidden: Basically, women are not inclined to truth.

The thought shocked him. He usually kept his prejudices buried.

They sat silently at a corner table in the quiet little bar. At midnight, Kendall knew, it would be busy, noisy, smoky, drunken. But at the cocktail hour it was somnolent, which was why he had chosen it. He would have preferred talking in her apartment, which he remembered as a place of quiet, impersonal charm. Neat. But this time he hadn't been asked inside. When he rang the downstairs bell she had answered over the house-phone system that she would be right down.

The half-snow, half-rain had stopped, and it was still and cold in the streets, but in the little bar it was warm and pleasant. As he sat in the warm, dim room he didn't know where to start, or even why he was trying. He felt confused and, ridiculously, lonesome.

She wasn't helping. As she sat looking down into her drink, which she hadn't touched, her face was entirely remote. She was, he thought with surprise, immensely attractive, almost beautiful. The realization surprised him because he had not recognized the fact the first time he met her. But that was because she had been so contained, so expressionless, so uncommunicative—neat and unostentatious and impersonal, like her apartment.

The lack of ostentation had been a shock to him. He had gone there expecting a siren, and he had found a nun. At the time he had thought it was an act, and he had been annoyed and rude. Now, when he had proof of how different she *could* look, he decided, illogically, that it had not been an act.

Two months before, Marta Wentwirth's hair—clean-looking, shiny, dark-brown hair—had been confined by its own slight waves into a coif. If he had been asked he would have said it was long hair, because it had fallen into a precise, rather tight roll at the back that looked almost like the buns women sometimes wore when he was a small boy. Now—disarranged, almost disheveled—it revealed itself as being less than shoulder length, and the result of its disarray was unexpectedly dramatic. She looked as if she had been standing in a wind, a high wind, and hadn't been in the least concerned by what it had done to her or her hairdress. Her features were small, and, he had thought, not very interesting. But now the dark aureole of hair lent drama to them, so that her too-short nose became an intensely feminine feature, and her full but small mouth seemed larger.

She looked up from the glass and stared at him, a thoroughly inimical stare. She had very large, dark-gray eyes, and he remembered that they had somehow reminded him of Quakers—a strange analogy, but their color and air of peace and straightness of gaze had evoked it. Now they were like the sky outside—still and cold, with the knowledge and forlornness of winter.

In view of his usual diffidence and fear of personal invasion—especially at the hands of a woman—he was surprised to find himself wishing she would be warmer, more receptive, less antagonistic. He wanted—what? Understanding? Forgiveness? Or was he simply looking, in a practical way, for a lead to the explanation of the messenger and the phone call?

Well, no matter what his motive, he had to start.

"Suppose I try to tell you how it happened?" He paused. It was the wrong start, he thought. He sounded hesitant, apologetic, and he had really had no cause to change his mind about her. But he couldn't stop there. "There was no reason not to believe him, no reason for him to lie." It was hard going, in the face of his own indecision and the glare of those stormy eyes, but after a minute he stumbled on.

"He was so quick, so—gay, nimble, mercurial. He talked,

and I didn't even have to ask questions. *Genesis of Treason* is going to make a lot of money for me, I guess, and a reputation, too. But it's not my story; it's his. Even the title is his."

V

Kendall had been surprised by the guards, the bars. He had had a vague idea that military prisons were different in some way. And then when they let him into Hollister's cell, Hollister's army fatigues lent him a prison-garb air.

But he was a shining man. He gave the cell a movie-like mood; for no reason except his presence it looked like a set. Kendall had the fleeting thought that Hollister was standing in a baby spot, a pink and golden beam. But, of course, the beam was merely a ray of sun as it broke through the barred window behind Hollister. Kendall himself, as he stood at the door, was in comparative darkness.

Hollister was smiling as they clanged the door behind Kendall, and, as always, his smile trembled so near the edge of laughter that when you thought about it later your mind supplied a chuckle to the soundless gesture.

He said, "You're Kendall, and you're a reporter on the *Courier*, and how in hell did you ever manage to get through my personal Gestapo?"

Kendall said slowly, "I'm not on the *Courier;* I'm a free-lance assigned by them."

Hollister had a quick way of speaking. Without actually interrupting, he leaped in with astonishing speed. "You're *from* the *Courier?*" he asked, almost before Kendall had closed his mouth.

"Yes."

"So it's a difference in prepositions. You're a purist. And honest. And maybe not so bright. I guess that's why they let you through."

It was foolish to give this boy's words any weight, Kendall knew. But his own incredulity at having been chosen for the job had, in the usual pattern of unconceited men, only added to his lack of self-esteem. He didn't move and his face didn't change, but his corner of the cell seemed darker. The boy laughed.

Hollister was slender, almost too slender. Although he was Kendall's height—a little under six feet—he looked shorter, and compared to Kendall's stocky breadth, very slight. But for all his thinness, he had good shoulders. As Kendall inspected him, Hollister raised his hand and pushed it through his blond curls. It was a gesture Kendall was to come to know well. Hollister performed it carelessly, not quickly, and yet it had the quality of caged energy. Hollister never sat down; but he never paced nervously. He was never quite still; but he was never jerky or forthrightly energetic. Yet it was clear to Kendall, and would have been to any onlooker, that he was as tense as an overwound jumping jack or, in his not infrequent venomous moments, as a rattlesnake just before the forward strike. The hand passing through the hair loosened the spring in the jack, diverted the strike of the snake, just in time to make the moment bearable.

Hollister interrupted the inspection. "Well," he asked, arrogantly but not unpleasantly, "what do you see?"

Kendall sat down on a stool in the corner beside the door and looked up at him, surprised by the vitality of the man, by his youth, by his arrogance—wondering just what he was seeing, weighing his impression and his answer.

But Hollister was not a man who waited. "Whatever you *think* you see," he added, "there's one thing about me you don't know: no other civilian has *really* seen me, no other civilian has *really* known me. I've only been me—the me you're talking to—for the last few weeks. So you're in a unique position."

That's when Kendall decided Francis Burton Hollister was crazy. Hollister had been in the New York cryptographic office of the Army for four years, and his life before that time was an open book. But later, when Kendall talked to people outside, he realized there was a good deal of truth in the claim. And then, for the first of the many switches to follow, he decided Hollister was sane.

Hollister moved the few feet across his cell, pushing his hair off his forehead. He was extraordinarily graceful. "Now, let's see. They told me your name, that you are a reporter, that you are associated with the *Courier*. They told me that I am not to discuss the details or the exact nature of my, uh, supposed crime—which is a laugh, since I wouldn't discuss it even at the trial—and that you have been put on your honor not to permit me to do so if I should suddenly decide to change my mind." He laughed. "So I can add to my few facts that you are considered to be a man of honor.

"Now, why are you here? Well, it would seem that you are going to attempt to describe me, my present character and appearance, or my past—before the trial—to the public." He paused and raised a humorous eyebrow at Kendall. "Right?"

Kendall said, "More or less." He was content to wait, to look and to listen.

"Now that presumes great insight on your part. Do you have great insight?"

Kendall shook his head.

"Well, then, are you a trained psychoanalyst?—I hasten to add that insight and psychoanalysis are by no means the same thing."

Kendall said, "I am not a psychoanalyst."

"Perhaps that's just as well for you." Hollister moved to the opposite side of the little cell and leaned lightly against the wall. He was glowing with energy and a suddenly malicious humor. "—Because the psychoanalyst they assigned to me is such an unhappy man as a result of the experience that I think he's going to have to go through a personal analysis all over again. He came to the conclusion that I am a megalomaniac, but even he realized that that wasn't very profound or comprehensive. And he never got any further." His smile broadened. "I confused him."

The smile turned into a laugh, and the laugh held real delight. And then, with a speed Kendall had never before witnessed in human emotions, Hollister turned completely serious. He regarded Kendall levelly and said, "Well, what *is* your qualification? What is it *you* can see or interpret that will make a story worth reading? It seems to me your article is doomed."

Kendall went along. He said, "I wouldn't entirely agree, but I do see what you mean. From your point of view."

The answer obviously didn't please Hollister. He became didactic: "You cannot see my point of view; you never will. And you *don't* see what I mean. Now, look: You are here because the military got scared. It doesn't take much to scare them, but this time they are quite right to be frightened. I have become a *cause célèbre,* and they are stuck with me. The American public is pretty damned foolish—like nothing in the world quite so much as a bunch of cows. But a bunch of cows on the rampage is a frightening thing. Any mass of animals moving together is frightening and powerful. Too bad the Americans don't know how to move together more often. Because of that inability the King of Babylon shall certainly come and destroy this land, and shall cause to cease from thence man and beast."

My God, Kendall thought, he's not a little off; he's completely crazy. He's—

Hollister said, "I'm not crazy, you know. That's a quote from the Bible. And I'm not a religious fanatic. But they've supplied me with a Bible, and I've got plenty of time to read." He waved toward a table beside the narrow, built-in bunk. "Interesting reading, too. That quote was from Jeremiah. The King of Judah had burned a roll—that was a book—and the Lord was angry. It's quite a story. Of course, Mr. Gershwin had a point, too: 'The things that you're liable—To read in the Bible—'Tain't necessarily so.'

"Anyway, where was I?" His hand went through his hair, and he looked puzzled. Then he said, "Oh, yes. The Army let the public see they thought the public stupid and not to be trusted, and the public didn't like it. Also, very nearly outright, the brass hats said, 'The hell with Hollister's rights. We, the Army, say he hasn't got any.' And now they're stuck with their highhandedness, and they don't know how to keep press and public off their necks." He smiled. "So you are to be the sop. You are an honest man and just as stupid as the rest of the American public, and they'll instinctively believe your report. So you have been chosen to tell them about me. To prove that I am not incommunicado—I am not incommunicado! *I*—who haven't seen a human being out of uniform since the second they picked me up!

"But what can you say? Without my active help, what is there to say? If we are not going to discuss my alleged act of treason—and we are not—about all you can do is describe how I look. And a picture does that better."

He walked over and stood in front of Kendall, and Kendall saw, with a small feeling of shock, that Hollister was entirely in command of himself. Also, as he looked soberly down at Kendall, he seemed, for the first time, to look his age. He was twenty-six years old—only eight years younger than Kendall—but until that moment he had looked like a boy of twenty.

He stood quietly, holding Kendall's gaze, and then he said slowly, "I'll make a bargain with you. I'll give you a story, a series of stories, that will make good reading. They will not whitewash me—in fact we'll never discuss my possible guilt or innocence—but they will be an interesting report on a fabulous person—me. I assume you are a good writer; notwithstanding my comments I realize you would not have been chosen for this assignment if you didn't have qualifications. So presumably you will do me justice." He paused. Then he added imperiously, "You will call the story, article, book—whatever you write—'Genesis of Treason,' and you will report faithfully most of what I say."

He stopped and waited. Kendall said nothing. After a minute, Hollister asked sharply, "Agreed?"

Kendall said slowly, "To a degree. I am here for the express purpose of reporting what you say, so that part is easy. I must, of course, put some interpretations on it. You will probably never see the finished piece—certainly not before it is published—so you must mean to take me on faith. And if you say anything the Army does not wish to have said it will be taken out of my hands anyway, since it will be carefully censored. You understand that, Lieutenant Hollister?"

Hollister walked across the room. When he turned and faced Kendall he was smiling again. "I've been—demoted, you know." He laughed. "Call me Buddy; everybody does. Of course I understand. I think that's just swell." He was twenty again, a restless twenty that moved ceaselessly around the small room.

"We'll start by my telling you about a woman. We can't say she is responsible for my downfall, because we are not saying I've had a downfall. Let's just say that the gods, to avenge themselves, sometimes grant us our desires. She was my desire, and the gods are avenged. And from your point of view a story about a woman is a good beginning, because Americans are hopelessly romantic, and because if it weren't for her—" He left the suggestion there, laughed, shrugged. "Her name is Marta Wentwirth. Her heart is a great big red brick. She's distant and aloof and inexpressive, and I've loved her for years. It was when I was leaving her apartment that I was picked up. Something of myself died there with her. I doubt that she knew it.

"It reminds me of that story I mentioned in Jeremiah. The King of Judah was setting before a fire on the hearth 'in the ninth month'—I was picked up as we left her apartment on September first, you know. . . ."

VI

Kendall made interlocking rings on the table with the damp bottom of his glass. After a long pause, he looked up at Marta Wentwirth and said, "The rest was substantially what you read in the first installment in the *Courier.* It was all about you, and his mixed feelings toward you. He never said you were implicated in his case or his conviction—"

"But he implied it." The words were rapid, but her voice was held carefully low. "Or, at least, *you* implied it. And since he could have had no reason for such an implication, unless he was crazy—and in my two brief meetings with him he didn't seem crazy—it seems more likely that you made the whole thing up."

Kendall leaned back against the padded divan and said evenly, "Now, why would I do that?"

"I don't know. Maybe because it makes a good story. As far as I can be dispassionate about it, I'll admit it does make a good story. In fact, since it was pure fiction to me, I thought it was all quite interesting."

The bitterness in her eyes hadn't abated, and they now seemed to grow darker, as if the threatened storm was imminent. It was obvious that she was in a rage mixed, perhaps, with despair, and the carefully even voice was her attempt at control. She said, "Also, I'm no lawyer, but it seems to me that you have very cleverly stayed this side of libel. You haven't directly accused me of anything, and I'm sure a lawyer will throw up his hands."

He said, "The *Courier*—"

She brushed her still full glass to the side with an abrupt gesture. Some of the liquid sloshed on the tabletop. She ignored it and leaned toward him. Her eyes were almost black. She said rapidly, "Now, look, Mr. Kendall, I don't like being here. I agreed to see you only because you offered me—something. First you said there was an explanation of your behavior. That wouldn't have interested me for a second—an explanation would merely make you feel better, presuming you have a conscience, which I doubt—but then you mentioned 'extricating me.' If you do have a conscience, and it carries you that far, then I'm interested."

Her bitterness and anger went far beyond scorn. There was something frighteningly convincing about her. Kendall felt cold. He said, "Yes, I have an explanation. Look: I was assigned to do a character piece, a mood piece, on Hollister. There was no question of my reporting facts. Actually, I was specifically forbidden to. No mention of exactly what Hollister had done was to be permitted—even if I got an inkling. Incidentally, I never did. The only other specification was that if I found it necessary to take an attitude either way, I was to assume Hollister guilty, not innocent. After all, he had been tried by the United States Army, found guilty, and sentenced to thirty years in prison. As the *Courier* pointed out, I could hardly flout that unless I had facts."

Her clenched hand moved restlessly on the tabletop, and he added quickly, "This is not irrelevant. The point is right there: I wasn't required to *check up* on what Hollister said because I wasn't making a report of the kind of facts that needed checking. I wasn't a reporter in the crusading sense; I was a reporter in the character sense. Do you see?"

She had stopped moving and was sitting rigidly still. She regarded him levelly, and he wondered what she was thinking of him as she stared at him. Of his appearance. Nothing reassuring, he thought, with his usual self-deprecation. Physically, a big man, a strong man. But in manner —unpretentious, diffident, almost shy. He had a high forehead that went smoothly down to heavy eyebrows; he did not hold his eyes completely open and he usually seemed to be looking up at people from under the thick black brows. The gesture was an unconscious defense against intrusion; without conscious decision, he believed that the formidable brows succeeded in overshadowing the peaceful forehead.

Well, whatever she thought of him, it caused no change in the cold impersonality of her voice. "Then why," she asked, "did you come to see me? If you weren't looking for facts? And, having come, why did you proceed as if you hadn't talked to me at all?"

Why had he gone to see her? He spoke slowly, as much for his own benefit as hers. "I saw Hollister five times—

spent maybe four hours with him over a period of two weeks. He was so contradictory—sane, insane; humble, grandiose; old, young; clever, stupid; religious, profane—that I began to get confused. The more you try to fill in a confused personality on paper, the more thoroughly you yourself must understand him. So I needed other views. Then, when I talked to a few people who had known him before the trial, I was, at first, more confused than ever. It turned out that the Hollister I was visiting hadn't existed for anyone before the trial. That's when I began to understand what he had meant about not being known to anyone.

"Hollister, people told me, was a pleasant, good-looking, colorless young man. That's just about all anyone had to say. The very fact that they used so few words in their description of him was a tipoff. If I started right now to describe the Hollister I met, I'd use a million adjectives; I'd interpret, interpolate, contradict. I'd get lost in the complexities, and the picture I'd draw would be brilliant, so brilliant that it would dazzle you and you would be a little blinded—wouldn't be able to see it clearly."

She was looking at him with a kind of frigid, clinical interest, and he became acutely aware of having revealed a passionate interest in Hollister, the extrovert. He felt undressed.

He said hurriedly, "So I finally went to see you. I figured you *certainly* would know him. From his story, you knew him better . . ." His voice trailed off.

The clinical interest was still there. She quoted: "'You

finally came to see me.' If you felt that I was such an obvious key to Hollister's character, why 'finally,' Mr. Kendall? Why not first?"

He stared at the table.

Her voice rose a trifle, as if all her will power could not keep it completely under control. "Because you had prejudged me? Because you didn't like me before you met me? Because you thought—what was Hollister's phrase?—'I was responsible for his downfall'? No matter how much he damned me by disclaiming it?"

He didn't look at her. "Perhaps," he mumbled.

"All right," she said coldly, "that makes a kind of sense. But then you *did* come to see me, and I told you, without hesitation, what little I knew. I thought you were basically a gentle man but rather hostile at the moment—I didn't know why. I got the impression that you just didn't like women. Why didn't you tell me *then* you didn't believe me, and give me a chance to defend myself?"

"Well"—he hesitated—"there were two reasons. The first" —he could feel the heat coming down from his forehead, and he hated the obviousness of his embarrassment—"doesn't reflect very much credit on me. You see, I had never worked for the *Courier* before. Nor for any publication nearly as—as greatly esteemed. I was flattered at having been chosen for the assignment. It was a great chance. When I saw you I had already turned that first installment in. Long before. In fact I had already given them the first three or four parts. And they were very pleased with them. Very pleased. They say the piece is going to create a sensation. My book publishers think it will hit the top of the nonfiction list and stay there. So—I was human. I didn't want to disturb things. And especially—we come to my second reason—" He stopped, and then went doggedly on, "because I didn't believe a word you said."

She said bitterly, "So Buddy Hollister was right. He implied that you considered yourself loaded with insight, and he laughed at you and shamed you into denying it. But you did consider yourself qualified to sit in judgment on me, without even telling me I was being judged."

"No, no," he said defensively and earnestly. "I arrived at my conclusion purely by logic. Think it over, Miss Wentwirth, unemotionally, logically. Hollister had been convicted. Appeal had been denied. He was stuck, and all the public furor had done him no good and showed no signs of ever doing him any good. He did not accuse you of having committed any crime, so he was not trying to shift legal blame to you. He merely said he had known you well. If he were lying, he would have nothing to gain by the lie. I thought"—Kendall's words came more slowly—"his motive was vindictiveness, a desire to cause you trouble, to see to it that you didn't get off scot-free. But that, in itself, was substantiation of his story. Who is vindictive to an utter stranger?"

"Apparently you are, Mr. Kendall."

He tried not to feel the lash; he went on as if he hadn't heard. "But when I came to you, what did you say? That you and Hollister *were* utter strangers. That you had met Hollister at a cocktail party; he had called you two days later; you had agreed over the phone to go to dinner with him that evening of September first; he had arrived at your apartment at six; the two of you had left the apartment at twenty minutes after six; and the authorities had met you in the doorway and had arrested Hollister. In other words, you claimed that you had spent a total of about two hours in all with Hollister.

"In the newspaper reports—if you can call those skimpy little pieces 'reports'—all that was ever said about you was that the Army had exonerated you of any connection with Hollister's treasonable acts. When I saw you, you mentioned wistfully that you found the public mention of your name very embarrassing, but you were trying to proceed on the premise that a chance meeting with someone who became notorious could happen to anyone. You said that people had been very kind and apparently had understood the incidental quality of your connection with Hollister.

"Well, Miss Wentwirth, I put it to you: who had something to gain by lying? What could it profit Hollister to make up a lie about knowing you for years, about loving you, about never forgetting you? But, on the other hand, wasn't it of vital importance to you to say *you* didn't know *him?*"

Marta Wentwirth was looking down into her glass again. Since her back was poker straight and her shoulders rigid, the forward motion came from the nape of her neck. The pose drew a beautiful line. The dark hair fell forward, obscured her ears, outlined her cheekbones . . .

She looked up without warning and caught his gaze,

and their surprise was mutual. Feeling safe, unobserved, he had been looking at her without his usual beetling upward glance, and she saw him full on for the first time—the full, unguarded, rather handsome face of a gentle, shy, lonesome, retiring man.

His sense of surprise arose from her lack of anger. The gray eyes were wide and somber, but the cold thundercloud was gone.

He looked quickly across the room, feeling ridiculous, furiously angry with himself, his lack of poise, his sense of having been caught . . . When he brought his head back, properly dropped at the chin so his protective armor was in place, she was staring into her glass.

She said, and her voice was in a lower register, "All right, Mr. Kendall. It makes some sense. But it doesn't help me one bit, and it doesn't whitewash you, in my eyes. You still accused me in public print of—undefined crimes—without giving me any chance to defend myself. But—" Her head came up—"why come to me now? Not belated conscience, is it?"

He would have liked to say yes. He would have liked to absolve her of everything. He would have liked to— But a dogged honesty was an integral part of him. "No. Not very good sense, either. It's just that I'm no longer sure. Not about you, specifically, but about any part of it. When I got finished with that article I was—satisfied. I had painted a picture of a man. The man was confused, but the *picture* wasn't. I had shown his reactions to his boyhood, his young manhood, his manhood; to his father, his mother, his—girl. I implied that he was guilty, and I showed, by indirection, how he got that way. It was truly the *genesis* of treason. The reader understood Buddy Hollister, as much as I or any sane person could understand someone as emotionally unstable as he."

Kendall paused, and then added tonelessly, "And then he killed himself."

He stared at her, but he didn't see her or anything but his own confusion. "That was absolutely contrary to my version of Hollister's character—the version I was proud of having drawn clearly and concisely. Sure, Hollister was capable of suicide, and he no doubt took great delight in outwitting his guards, in managing to accomplish the act itself. But the Hollister I knew—and reported to several million people—had to have a great reason for killing himself, a shining cause, according to his own standards. Patriotism, perhaps. Communism. Any ism. But *not* despair. Never anything so negative as despair. It was—just impossible."

In the first outward expression of his misery and self-doubt, he looked full face at her, not aware of it. In confession, his guard fell around him. "The first thing I ever felt I had done really well, and I had done it all wrong."

He didn't hear her whisper at first through his numbness, and when he looked questioningly at her, although she raised the whisper slightly it still had no voice behind it: "Could *they* have done it?"

It brought him out of his preoccupation with a shock. "Oh, no!" Then he subsided and added, "Oh, if by 'they' you mean an alien group, Communists or such, they couldn't have got to him. He was guarded—really guarded."

"I—didn't mean an—alien group."

The shock was less the second time. But still—

"No, no!" he said earnestly. "You mustn't think such a thing! I caught hints of it in the papers, too. When we admit to such a suspicion we destroy ourselves. The Army has been stupid, stupid if only in permitting themselves to get into a position where such a thought could arise and persist. But stupidity, mismanagement—why, they're basic, fundamental, in a democracy. When you've got a lot of people with a lot of different ideas running *anything*—to say nothing of a vast country—sure you get stupidity, waste, all sorts of minor sins. But not the major sin. The Army didn't silence Hollister. No. I guess I was simply wrong in my interpretation of the guy."

He paused as a thought caught up with him. Her suggestion, disapprove as he might, was tuned to an acceptance of him, as a person, as a reporter. He had erected a structure to prove he was in error; she had sought a weapon strong enough to knock it down. In spite of her anger.

It was nice of her.

He repeated firmly, in an effort to get on firmer ground, "No. Hollister undoubtedly committed suicide. But that fact has been burning painfully in my mind. And then today something else happened that also seems inexplicable. A phony messenger, purporting to be from the *Courier*, showed up at my apartment for a copy of *Genesis of Treason.* Then someone called—equally phony—and tried to pry a copy out of me. Either dodge would have worked if I had had a copy."

"You checked?"

"I checked."

"You reported this to Army security?"

"Why, no." He stared at her. "Why should I do that? They passed the story. Presumably they don't care who I give it to. That's just what makes it seem so inexplicable. What does anyone want with it? And what's their hurry?"

"Your art?" she murmured. There was humor but no sarcasm in her voice.

"I thought of that. Spent a whole ten seconds basking in it." He smiled at her—his very rare smile that, although he didn't know it, rivaled Hollister's in warmth and contagious good humor. "A delightful idea, but I'm afraid I can't go along with it."

"And what good— What did you think *I* could supply toward a solution?"

He hesitated. "I didn't know," he said finally.

"You thought—" She stared at him. "Good heavens, did you think I'd confess to being mastermind of a spy ring, and solve it all for you?"

"No. Well, of course not. But—" What had he hoped? "Perhaps something a little like that," he mumbled, feeling foolish.

She smiled slightly, but let the admission pass without comment, and they sat quietly, antagonism no longer charging the air. When she spoke, her voice was low, slow, ruminative: "It comes to this—you have been set back in your search for pride, wounded in your self-esteem. I can understand that, but it rather annoys me that I can. That I feel a little sympathy. Because there is no sympathy in you."

He was shocked. "Of course there is!"

"Really?" The quick glance from under her eyelashes was entirely ironical. "Look—you have a problem. I accept it. I am sorry for it. Even though I didn't create it. On the other hand, I have a problem. You *did* create it. Do you know what it is? Have you tried for a second to understand it, its implications, to put yourself in my position? My job? My friends? I have taken an indefinite leave of absence from my office, under the pretext of illness, which no one believed for a moment. I had the quite terrible feeling that they were relieved to have me go. I can't believe that I'll ever have the courage to go back, or that they'd want me if I tried to. Have you thought of my parents—in a small upstate town? The *Courier* has excellent circulation up there. Have you any conception of how—" She stopped, as if overwhelmed by the re-estimate of her situation, by the hopelessness of the recital.

He had a sudden, pounding headache. This was pointless. What good could he do her or she, him? Would it help to confess that he had a very good idea of what she was going through? Would it help to say that he had felt justified: or, perhaps, righteous? What good did it do for him to feel defensive, badgered, when the situation hadn't really changed? His logic was still good, and if her personality got through to him— Well, wasn't that the way Hollister had felt about her?

He looked at his wrist, but found he had left his watch home again. Still, it must be seven. "Shall we go have some dinner?" he asked.

Then he was astonished. How many times in your life, he wondered, do you speak completely without volition? And why wasn't she also surprised by the invitation? She was looking at him in silence, impassively. In spite of all his analogies to Quakers and winter nights, the only real difference in her appearance, he decided, was the hairdress. That made all the difference, though.

He said, "You should always wear your hair that way."

That time he had surprised her. Her eyebrows lifted and a slight flush relieved the natural paleness of her face. Then she looked past him at the mirror set into the wall. She stared into it unself-consciously and without fussing. She didn't comment that she was disheveled; she didn't produce lipstick or powder. She just looked.

Then she said, "It doesn't look—abandoned?"

"Perhaps. A little. But good."

"I see." Still staring into the mirror, she added, "There's something wrong with me, too."

Kendall thought, Too? Yes. Yes, he had given her that right.

"—I'm twenty-five, but I'm not alive. I have spent my twenty-five years avoiding—being alive." She looked at him with a touch of entreaty and then made a gesture of hopelessness with her hand, as if the explanation were beyond her.

He said, "I know. You simply concentrated on not looking abandoned."

She smiled.

VII

At ten-thirty, as he entered the crotchety little elevator in his building, he realized that he had had a pleasant evening.

They had gone to a small Italian restaurant a few blocks from the bar, and had had some very bad wine with their dinner. They had been rather speechless for the first half-hour, but it hadn't been an uncomfortable silence. And eventually they had talked a good deal.

That conversation—the fact of it—was rather surprising as he looked back on it now. And he thought it likely that she, too, rarely filled in the details of her existence so freely for a stranger. Perhaps, he thought, the unorthodox basis of their acquaintanceship, in creating its own peculiar stress, had distracted him from the more usual strain he experienced with women. Whatever the reason, he had given her his gnat's-eye view of the Second World War, and had told her something about the problems and satisfactions of life as lived by a free-lance writer. And she had filled him in on the advertising-agency business.

She was a copy writer—an occupation she openly considered insane, but which, he gathered, she did very well. He was intrigued by the impersonality of her comments. She had been with the same agency for almost four years, but she spoke of it with the detachment of a day-old employee. Or as if she normally observed it through a glass pane in its ceiling. He finally commented on that: "It doesn't get home to you, does it?"

"Get home?" She cocked her head to the side and asked the question half of herself, half of him.

"Concern you. Twist you. Keep you awake nights. Make you lose your sense of humor. Make you swear. Or—" He paused "—or give you any very great satisfaction, either."

She regarded him gravely, her eyes held rather wide. They were compellingly magnificent eyes, of a strange and indeterminate color. The hell with Quakers and winter and storms, he thought; they were like—

She said, "I don't get worked up, no. Ulcers are considered a badge of honorable arrival in the agency business. I think that's pretty ridiculous, don't you?"

"Yes, I suppose so. Well, of course."

The wide eyes fixed him levelly, but they held a faint trace of a question. She said with a gentle insistence that was surprising in one so uninsistent, "But you understand the ulcers, don't you? Sympathize?"

"Well—" He wasn't entirely sure what they were talking about. Her grave manner seemed out of proportion. He said, "Look. This is a sort of silly discussion. Ulcers are silly—unless you have 'em. To worry and strain yourself into having them is silly, I guess. My 'sympathy,' if that's what it is, is simply an understanding of the intensity, the passion, some people can put into their work, into anything they do. They're alive—so they care; they care—so they stew; they stew—so, ulcers." He nodded his head with a quod-erat-demonstrandum acceptance.

"Oh. And detachment? What about detachment?" She still seemed to be asking a question that was somewhere below the level of the surface conversation.

"The most admirable quality in the world," he assured her. "Conducive to clear vision, clear action." He wondered if he really believed that. He added, "And beyond the reach of most mortals."

She laughed, and he saw her even, rather small teeth for the first time. They gave her a very young quality—a new facet in his picture of her. Through the laugh, she said, "That makes me practically immortal, doesn't it?"

Yes, he had enjoyed the evening—and that was surprising, not only because he had approached it full of inner doubt and outward confusion and because he had been on the defensive through the beginning of it, but because Kendall did not normally enjoy cocktails and dinner with young women. He tried. Or he had tried, up to a few years before. But it never worked for him. He became, in the presence of women, a less likable man. He was at all times withdrawn, self-conscious, monosyllabic. But men usually got through his barriers, and came to like and enjoy him. No woman ever got through. Although he told himself the situation was entirely his own fault, he did not really believe that. His personality changed because he feared them. And not without sound reason.

As the elevator drew to a jerky stop and he let himself

out on his landing, a cold fact arose out of the pleasant mist and chilled him. Outside of beauty, an interesting, if remote, personality, a charm and seeming integrity that had warmed him, there was no reason to believe Marta Wentwirth any more now than there had been at five o'clock. She had not added a fact, she had not made an additional protest, she had not in any way changed the situation—except by seeming increasingly sympathetic and attractive.

He had a bitter taste in his mouth as he put his key into the lock. Hollister had obviously taken him in—given him an entirely misleading view of his personality; had Marta Wentwirth managed it too?

"The moon is not round for long." He wondered where the unbidden thought came from, and simultaneously recognized it as a comment of Buddy Hollister's. As he stepped into his inner hall, he found himself adding Marta Wentwirth to Buddy Hollister, and resenting their influence on his thoughts.

When he switched on the lights and the insane turmoil arose to greet him, he experienced very little surprise. He should have known it; he should certainly have foreseen it.

As he wandered through the ransacked, chaotic apartment, his prime emotion was annoyance with his own stupidity. Someone had wanted a script; they had made two tries at getting it; the next step had been clearly indicated if he had simply thought it through.

On the dresser in the bedroom where he had left it was his watch. An excellent, expensive watch. And nothing else seemed to be missing, either. It was quite clearly not a matter of robbery, and of course he hadn't thought it was.

Still, you couldn't ignore it. You had to do something. He called the police.

The desk sergeant was bored; the robbery detail was bored. Kendall eventually became irritated.

He said to some man named Vincent, "Now, look, Mr. Vincent . . . All right, *Sergeant* Vincent, I've admitted that nothing is missing—and 'admitted' is a funny word for you to have pushed me into using—and I don't give a damn what you do about it, so please stop asking me what I expect you to do about it. Don't do anything. I don't care. But are you suggesting that I shouldn't have called you? Shall I hang up? It's all right with me—"

He listened to Vincent for a few impatient moments and then he said, "Yes, of course I'll be awake. I'll wait for you here."

Sergeant Vincent, a tall, gaunt, dissatisfied-looking young man, arrived in about twenty minutes. He was wearing a shiny brown suit, and an overcoat that looked as if it had been polished to match. He had two men with him, one also in civilian clothes, the other a uniformed patrolman.

They wandered through the apartment, Vincent looking annoyed. They examined the front door, and Vincent muttered that there was certainly no mystery about the means of entry.

Kendall noticed the raw wood then. The door had been

expertly forced, so neatly and with so little waste motion that the lock had not been sprung and his key had still worked.

Vincent's questions combined insult with contempt. Nothing was missing? (Implied corollary: nothing was worth stealing.) Search for a manuscript? (Implied corollary: how conceited can you get?)

But as he left, after fifteen minutes of the futile, desultory questioning, he paused in the doorway and said contemplatively, "A manuscript? Robert Kendall? Oh, yes."

Kendall thought sardonically that his first touch of fame, the first recognition of his name as belonging to a remotely public figure, had been played to the lowest. Vincent recognized it—yes; but he made it clear that he was not impressed.

After the door had closed, Kendall dragged the mattress back onto the bed, tossed some sheets and blankets over it, and slipped somewhere in between the layers. The bed was no more confused than his life, he thought. The far-fetched analogy amused him, but wryly.

On that note of confusion and self-deprecating amusement, he went to sleep.

VIII

He said to Major Windham, "There was no question of my being 'taken in' by Miss Wentwirth. What's more important, there would have been no danger if I *had* been taken in—whatever you mean by that. The articles are written; the series has started to run. I couldn't do much changing if I wanted to. I don't want to. Miss Wentwirth didn't ask for a carbon. And I don't have one, anyway. I took her to dinner, came home to this—this vandalism, called the police, and went to bed. That's it."

Windham was still leaning forward, his arms on his knees, and as he spoke Kendall slowly began to feel that the pontifical tone was natural—not affected, and not a true indication of character; that Windham probably took himself too seriously and probably lacked humor, and that those qualities combined to give an unfortunate impression. But something else—a basic kindness, a vast earnestness, an incorruptible tenacity—were really the keynotes on which he functioned.

He said, "Mr. Kendall, would you mind telling us why you saw Miss Wentwirth?"

A little pause followed the question, and he explained rather quickly, "It's a—a random question. We are seeking —admittedly quite blindly—for a starting point." The vision of the gleaming Hollister invaded the room, and he added, "—a new starting point."

Kendall had no desire to stumble through the explanation he had tried to make to Marta Wentwirth—that he was a man in search of salvation, who had somehow been thwarted again. He said shortly, "I thought Marta Wentwirth might clear things up for me. Hollister's suicide had made me unsure of my picture of him, of the portrait I had drawn."

Gregory said, "That's very astute."

Kendall looked at him from under his eyebrows. "Astute of me to recognize my own inadequacy?"

"No, no." Gregory looked rather surprised. "Astute of you to recognize that suicide was out of character for Hollister."

"You are implying that my portrait was correct then? That Hollister changed?"

"Why, no, Mr. Kendall. Adults don't change—rarely, at any rate, and not overnight." Gregory, Kendall thought, grew more interesting with the passing moments. So misleadingly boyish, so outwardly engaging, so contained and unimpetuous underneath. "No, Hollister had to have a strong motive for suicide, and since the only apparent result of his action was to speed things up, that must have been his motive. Very clever of him, too. But why did he want to speed things up? That's what we don't fully understand, and that's what worries us."

Kendall stared at Gregory. Then he said flatly, "I don't get it. Speed what up? What motive?"

"I'm surprised you haven't figured that out. The *Courier* scheduled your first installment for February fifteenth, didn't they? But it's not yet February and the first installment has already appeared. Why?"

"Why, because of—" Kendall's voice slowed—"because of Hollister's suicide. Because of his death and the reappearance of his name on the front pages of the newspapers, the piece became timely again—so timely they rushed into print . . ." He broke off as awareness overcame him.

Windham thrust his chin forward. "Exactly. That's exactly the point. Hollister asked his guards repeatedly when the articles would start running. No one gave the question a second thought. It sounded like the normal interest of an abnormal ego. But the day after someone gave him the February date, he managed the difficult job of hanging himself. He had no shoelaces, no belt, none of the—uh—conveniences. He tore his shirt into little shreds and braided it. There is evidence that the resulting rope broke under his weight twice, and that he painstakingly mended it. A very strong character, Francis Hollister, and a very determined one."

Gregory added, "And a shrewd one. Sheer intelligent journalism would dictate that the *Courier* rush in to take advantage of the news break. He forecast that neatly."

"Sure." Kendall had stopped twisting the belt of his robe. He was sitting on the edge of the couch, and, as in all moments of stress or excitement, his head was up and his eyes in full view. He was, as he sat there, in strange contrast to the man who had opened the door fifteen minutes before—younger, better looking, eager and appealing. "But the difference is a matter of only three weeks. So there must be something—"

"In the articles." Gregory nodded.

"With a deadline." Windham closed the conversation by putting his finger on the point. He was as pompous as ever, but Kendall had come rather to like him.

The major seemed to feel the change in the atmosphere, and, apparently on the strength of it, he ventured a question: "You more than half believed in his innocence, didn't you, Mr. Kendall?"

Kendall was startled, and as he struggled to form an answer, he was even more startled to realize that he had never permitted himself to probe that question. He talked the answer aloud, slowly.

"I never allowed myself to speculate consciously about his guilt or innocence. I was afraid it would divert me from my main intention—his character, not his acts. But of course I had feelings, unrationalized emotions. These emotions said that Hollister was guilty of something, but that the Army was guiltier—that they had made much of little; that the crime was probably not as important as it had been blown up to be; that they had been so unmitigatedly stupid in their handling of the situation that Hollister's—deviation—whatever it was—paled by contrast; that the Army—"

Kendall stopped abruptly. In his honest attempt to solve

his own complicated reaction to the question of Hollister's guilt or innocence, he had almost forgotten Windham's profession, and had entirely forgotten the man's obvious dedication to that profession. But Windham's expression and color suddenly and forcibly recalled those facts.

Windham had turned a slow, painful red, and he looked furious but frustrated. Into the lengthening silence, he emitted a strangled sound. It had no meaning. Then he collected himself to a degree, opened his mouth to the extent of a narrow slit, and said stiffly, "The Army–" He pulled a little air through the slit, and started again. "Shall we say, the Army did not handle the matter in the most advantageous manner. That you are not–entirely wrong –in your evaluation of the situation."

Kendall suddenly felt very sorry for the man. He fully understood the look of frustration on Windham's red face. Windham wanted to blast and disclaim, but he was too honest. Instead of a virulent denial of all Kendall had said –with an accompanying description of Kendall's forebears to the seventh generation–Windham had been forced to substitute Army doubletalk amounting to agreement.

Kendall could think of nothing to say. The apology he would have liked to offer would have been ridiculous.

Windham got his mouth open again. He said, "But there are excuses for us. Hollister's act was not a 'deviation,' not a bit of it. It was a sheer, outrageous act of high treason. That's reason number one for our–abrupt handling of him and of the situation: we had no sympathy for a proven traitor. And reason number two is that his crime involved our—uh—biggest secret. Something in which lies our hope for peace. Our most guarded . . ." He gestured helplessly.

Kendall said, "The H-Bomb."

Windham seemed thrown off base. "The H-Bomb?"

"At Seutaconawa, Montana."

"Ah, uh, yes."

Gregory smiled without apparent reason. Then he grew serious, and, with an almost imperceptible air of sympathy, took the burden of explanation off Windham's shoulders. "Don't you see, Mr. Kendall—? Because the Army was so desperately aware of the importance of the secret Hollister had got his hands on, they went into a panic of cover-up. They were guilty, in the final analysis, only of bad public relations."

Gregory stopped, seemed to consider, and then, with an air of decision, got to his feet. He offered cigarettes around, and lit one for himself. He picked up an ashtray and deposited it conveniently beside his chair. Then he settled down again and stretched his long legs comfortably out in front of him.

He said, "Major Windham and I decided, before we came over this morning, that you may be able to help us. However, we think it's vital that you trust us first, and to do that you will have to believe—unquestioningly—in the guilt of Francis Hollister. So we got permission to tell you what he did. Even now"—Gregory's youthful face permitted itself a deprecating smile—"it wasn't easy to get that permission. And yet I personally feel that as much of the story as we are going to tell you could have been given to the public. However, we have no control over that.

"This is what Francis Burton Hollister did." He crossed his legs at the ankles and slid deeper into his chair.

IX

"Hollister, we realize now," Gregory said, "was a sleeper —a member of the Communist Party whose whole life was dedicated to the one big moment. We've met them before, and I suppose we'll meet them again. But we've never had so clear-cut a case as Hollister's.

"He lived, until he was eighteen, with his widowed mother. They were in comfortable circumstances—Hollister's father died when he was ten, and left an adequate annuity. Hollister had no brothers or sisters. V-J Day fell around his eighteenth birthday, so he didn't get into that war. And then he missed the Korean War because, at eighteen, he went to West Point. He was appointed in the regular way, and he graduated in the regular way.

"Nothing very odd about that story, is there?" Gregory looked inquiringly at Kendall, who obediently shook his head.

"Well, there is." Gregory's long frame tensed and some of the iron determination underlying the boyish charm showed through as he strove to get his point over. "Nobody, but *nobody,* was ever as normal as Mr. Francis Burton Hollister. Everybody gets involved in something—a hobby, a club, a neighborhood gang, a debating society, a girl or series of girls, even some unusual quality in his schooling—great intelligence or great stupidity. But not

Hollister. He did go in for sports, but that was all. He never shone, and as you read the list of sports he participated in—practically every sport known in America—you begin to wonder at the will power such an all-round athlete must have exerted to keep from copping honors in *something*. But he didn't.

"Up until he was perhaps sixteen, his normality must have been a coincidence. Perhaps he was solicited for just the reason that it existed. Before his seventeenth year he had done a little better at sports than he did later, and—the single out-of-the-usual note—he had been a brilliant student. But by the time he was seventeen his grades had dropped until he was about a third of the way from the top. In everything. Note that: in *everything*. Who consistently draws down the same marks in every subject? Who isn't better in Math and worse in English, or vice versa? Answer: Mr. Hollister."

Gregory raised his right hand; it was clenched into a fist and it trembled with the intensity of the grip. "By God, Kendall, what a strange hold it is—to be able to get and guide a young man of promise to his triumphant death! To make him negate his birthright of intelligence, charm, handsomeness, the American chance at wealth, love, and pursuit of happiness—for what? A country he's never seen? A doctrine that has been constantly perverted for years? A group of people who lie so shamelessly that they are constantly being caught flat-footed—and then, when caught, lie again with open contempt?

"I can't overstate how far Hollister went to make himself nothing but a tool—a tool of unknown, unestimated usefulness. In addition to keeping his mental and physical prowess under wraps, he also succeeded in hiding his charm and even in disguising the excellence of his appearance. The honest eye of the camera caught his damned good-looking face and showed it for what it was, but do you know that when you press people who were acquainted with him for a description, they always seem surprised when they realize that he was good-looking?"

Kendall nodded. He had experienced that surprise in a number of the people he had talked with.

"Yes, you must have learned that. You must also have come to realize how blank and blah he had made himself to those acquaintances—he had no friends. And yet you should have seen him at the trial! Brilliance, wit, a pervading charm—I was permitted to sit in, and I shall never forget him. All those men knew him to be something they hated, and yet sometimes they were with him. He wasn't even pretending to innocence; he laughed at them. But occasionally they laughed with him."

"I can understand that. He tied me up in knots in his cell. I—" Kendall hesitated. Then he said firmly, "I am an inhibited man—silly word, but I don't know how else to phrase it. So I blamed it on myself. It's rather a relief to feel that I wasn't alone in being—fascinated." Kendall smiled, his infrequent, open, engaging smile.

Gregory seemed rather taken aback. Kendall didn't know it, but it was the quality of the smile that surprised Gregory—its Hollister-like charm. Gregory collected himself and said, "Well, there it was." He shook his red head of hair uncomprehendingly. "When he got into West Point they must have chosen his direction. He became almost imperceptibly better—not expert, but better than average—at those subjects that would lead him into the cryptographic section of G 2. When, at graduation, he showed his preference for that post, his admission was inevitable. He seemed to be just the kind of young man they look for. He got the job. And he worked there for almost four years."

Gregory lapsed into a momentary silence. Then he said broodingly, "His behind-the-scenes directors must have trusted him more than they usually trust their agents. It must have been left somewhat to his discretion as to what he was to do. Because what he eventually did was spur-of-the-moment, and they couldn't have predicted it. He simply saw his chance and took it. We are positive he wasn't siphoning out information before that big break. There was never a whisper about him, and later investigation disclosed the cleanest of records. It's clear they weren't jeopardizing his eventual value for a series of little bits and pieces.

"But the big moment came, and with lightning speed he saw it, estimated its value, and took it. And it's such a simple story. I guess the best way to get it across to you is to kind of set the scene, and the scene is more the story of a single character than a stage set. Did you know Brigadier General Myerson?"

"Orwell Myerson." Kendall nodded. "Knew *of* him. He died, didn't he, a few months ago?"

"Yes—he did. Well, he was the head of the whole works—the main secret-holder of the Army."

"I didn't know that."

"Few people did. We try, you know—the FBI, the Army, the Navy, the State Department—not to concentrate knowledge too tightly, but it's difficult not to."

"It's unforgivable." Windham came out of his brooding retirement to snap out the words. He looked guilty, as if a loan he had granted had blown up in the bank's face.

"No, Major, I wouldn't say that." Gregory was respectful but firm. "I would say rather, 'inevitable.' It's axiomatic that the more people know a secret, the less of a secret it is. So, inevitably, secrets become concentrated. General Myerson was a high concentration point.

"Myerson was a small man, five six or so, and he had a kind of simple face—round, almost plump, always pink. His eyes were light-blue, and his gray hair had thinned but not receded, so that it lay flat on his head like a new growth—like babies' hair. Altogether he looked rather like a baby—innocent and wide-eyed. An entirely misleading appearance.

"In his office, the main office of which held Hollister from nine to five, five and a half days a week, was a safe, and in the safe, coded to the hilt, were many of our biggest secrets. As nearly impregnable as a safe can be, and it remained impregnable throughout the Hollister affair."

"It shows you," Windham said bitterly. "You build an

impregnable safe, and then you take the stuff out of it and it might as well have been a tin box."

"In this instance, yes. Well, the safe was closed that afternoon, as usual, the office was neat, the general was at his desk, working. Before him was a single slip of paper, and on it was an incomprehensible set of diagrams that comprised an intricate code. No human being could read that code at sight, although the general came closest to being able to do so. What he was really expert at was being able to read the code after he had once deciphered it. It was like—" Gregory waved his hand rather helplessly and then said, "Well, say you give a man a hundred pieces of paper with a hundred different messages on them in classical Greek. He can't read Greek, but you explain what each message says. And then, a month later, when he picks up the papers, he can tell you what each one translates to. Well, the general decoded these special messages, courier-delivered, that no one else in the office ever saw, destroyed the transliteration, and then could read them without re-decoding. A valuable trick of memory.

"On that afternoon he had decoded the message before him into a mere couple of dozen words, and those words were lying in front of him in his own neat handwriting. Then he sent for Hollister.

"Why?" Gregory seemed to ask himself the question. Then he answered himself with an angry shake of the head. "We don't know. We'll never know. It couldn't have been about that specific code, because no one in the office ever had anything to do with it. Certainly not Hollister. Perhaps he wanted to ask a general question, and yet the message, when checked later, had been accurately decoded. Anyway, to make it even more annoyingly incomprehensible, Hollister, by rank and age, was not a person the general normally dealt with. Hollister probably hadn't been in that office twice in four years— So there's the scene."

Gregory stopped talking.

After a minute, Kendall said, "Yes. Well, what happened then?"

It was Windham who answered him. "Then the general dropped dead."

"Oh." It suddenly came through to Kendall as a vivid scene, the scene Gregory had tried to paint. The neat office, the cleared desk, the two sheets of paper. Behind the desk, the pink-and-blue little general, as neat as his office. In front of the desk, standing almost at attention, a subdued version of the Hollister he had known, looking not so blond, not so wise, but very proper and respectful. And then, without warning, the general's seizure, the pink face turning gray . . . he remembered now what he had read about Myerson's death: "suddenly, of a heart attack, in his sixty-first year" the papers had said, without further embellishment.

Kendall asked, "How long was Hollister in the office?"

Gregory smiled. "You ask good questions, Mr. Kendall— to the point. That was the first question asked in that hectic moment. And the answer was very disarming. Perhaps one minute, not more than two, was the general verdict. He came rushing out of the office looking terribly agitated, shouting, 'The General! The General!"

"Thereafter the matter was handled in a manner that reflects nothing but credit on the responsible people. In less than five minutes the—uh—security officer had taken over. In not much more than ten minutes a doctor had appeared and pronounced the general dead of a heart attack. There had been no haphazard rushing into the office; the general's secretary had handled that very efficiently. And so, beyond the death of a valued officer, everything seemed to be all right. The security officer—Windham, you had better explain the rest."

"Yes," Windham said, "because I was the security officer. Don't know why Gregory's being so secretive about that. Habit of our kind of training, I guess. I was the security officer, an ordinary security officer at the time, but a rather special one now because I saw that paper—and that gave me a knowledge I am not supposed to have, a knowledge that could undo a great deal of elaborate and expensive preparation if it were too widely known.

"When I first entered the general's office I thought everything was all right. But it's my job to make sure, so I dismissed that thought and proceeded as if the United States Army had just been handed over, lock, stock, and barrel, to the Russians in that room. The safe was closed—and even if you know exactly how to open it, it takes six minutes—so that angle was covered by the short amount of time that had elapsed. As for the rest of the room—my God, but it was neat. Even poor General Myerson's head, which had fallen forward onto the desk, didn't have a hair out of place. I couldn't see his face then, of course." An expression of pain quivered over Windham's rigidly held features. He added, "When the doctor arrived and I did see Myerson's face, I came to realize the office wasn't so peaceful, after all.

"However"—with obvious effort he dismissed the memory—"the desk was clear, too, except for the two pieces of paper Gregory has described to you. I bent over and looked at the coded one, which was unintelligible to me, of course, and then I circled around behind the general so I could see the paper that was facing him, a corner of it under his cuff. It didn't require very much thought to grasp the message, and it took only a second to realize that if that message leaked . . ." Windham shook his head.

"So I went into high gear. It was a simple setup. The general's secretary explained the circumstances, and it was instantly obvious that only he and Hollister had been in that room alone, and neither of them for much more than a minute. The secretary said that no one had gone around the desk while he was in there, and that he himself had not looked at the message.

"Then I sent for Hollister, a young man whom I knew slightly and thought very pleasant, and I put the question to him. He said he had not read the message either. The general had barely opened his mouth, he said, when he turned white, gasped a little, and fell forward on the desk."

Windham looked reflective. "I've lately come to the conclusion that the general may have died between the time he told his secretary to get Hollister and the time Hollister entered the room. Because Hollister didn't mention the terrible contorting of the face, and because human nature is such that one rushes to help a man who is dying—loosen his collar, chafe his hands, and so forth. But if he is lying there seemingly unconscious, a hand on his wrist tells the story, and then the inclination to give help gives way to the desire to *get* help. By lying, Hollister would account for the one minute he spent in the room. If he came in and found the general dead, then he should have been in there even less than a minute.

"Anyway, I accepted Hollister's story—I admit now that I accepted it without reservation, just as I did the secretary's—and I dismissed him. But I took the last precaution. After the necessary phone calls, telling the two proper authorities in this country what had happened and that I was holding—very gingerly, between two other pieces of paper—a message of vast importance, I fingerprinted the two papers. The coded piece was plastered with prints—the general's, two sets presumably belonging to the authors of the message, others—perhaps those of people who had originally handed the blank paper to the authors. But the decoded message was clean and clear. It contained a few smudgy prints of the general's and, in the upper right-hand corner, a single forefinger-pad mark."

Windham looked grim. "That was it," he said. "We keep all personnel prints on file, of course. It was Hollister's print. What had happened was perfectly clear: the slip of paper had been farther under the cuff, and he had carefully pushed it out far enough to see it.

"Even then it wasn't open and shut. He could have read the message, realized its import, and decided that it would be better to say he hadn't and keep the knowledge to himself. He could have panicked for any number of reasons. Perhaps, I told myself, he feared that simply having read the note constituted a court-martial offense.

"But when I sent for him, I was told he had gone. It was a half hour before closing time. He had never been known to leave before the official day was over. That frightened me.

"Then I had a piece of luck. Thank God." Windham made the words sound exactly like a thanksgiving, not an idle expression. "The man at the desk next to Hollister's was—well, you couldn't call him a friend; Hollister didn't have friends, but he was an acquaintance of long standing. Earlier that day he had heard Hollister make an appointment for dinner with a girl named Marta. This man had been at a cocktail party with Hollister a couple of days before and there had been a girl there named Marta Wentwirth. Thank heaven he remembered the name.

"Well, there was no certainty Hollister would keep that appointment, but—especially if he was guilty—it was a sound probability. He had left the office early; that was enough of a deviation. From now on it stood to reason that he would strive for complete normality, would try to live, appear, react, exactly as he would have if he were not in possession of the message. The chances were overwhelmingly in favor of his keeping that dinner engagement.

"So I called Gregory's office, he was assigned to help me, and we descended in force on Marta Wentwirth's neighborhood.

"And that's where we made our mistake." Windham looked at Gregory in an apologetic way.

Gregory said slowly, "Yes, I think we made a mistake. You see, Mr. Kendall, we were in an understandable panic. Hollister had been out of sight for almost an hour. We couldn't know what was happening during that time. We later came to the conclusion that he was simply trying to establish contact. He wasn't the kind of agent who reported regularly; as Windham explained, we don't think he ever really reported; he merely waited. For the big day; for the big assignment. So he probably spent the better part of that hour in telephone booths. But we didn't have that knowledge to reassure ourselves with at that time, and consequently we were scared to death. And so, as Windham puts it, we 'descended in force.' And, as a result, we were damned obvious.

"Hollister got to Miss Wentwirth's apartment building at about a quarter to six, and he stood in the doorway for almost fifteen minutes. I've never seen a man so nervous. He managed to light five cigarettes in fifteen minutes—and that's quite a trick. He paced. He looked up and down the street. He started down the few steps; he climbed them again. He ran his hands through his hair until it was a mass of curls. He was, it seems clear, waiting for his contact, but the contact never showed."

Windham said bitterly, "We had scared him away, of course. That must be the explanation. By the time Hollister got there we had our squadron—uh—deployed, behind doors and windows, not in obvious sight. But when we first arrived we rushed around like ants on an ant hill. The contact couldn't miss us, I suppose, so he kept right on going, simply walked through us."

Gregory said, "I think, Mr. Kendall, it must be clear to you now why the Army was guilty of such bad, er, press relations; such bad public relations in general. We had put an immediate makeshift tap on the Wentwirth telephone; there were no calls while Hollister was up there. We permitted no one in the building after he entered. We picked him up when he came out, less than half an hour later, and we took Miss Wentwirth, too. We were sure, at that point, that he had already transmitted the information. But in a very short time we changed our minds.

"Because Hollister, too, made a mistake. He was so absorbed in accomplishing his purpose he didn't realize that in that very determination he was defeating it. All he was interested in was some contact with the outside world. He didn't protest his innocence very much—occasional lip service, but he didn't really care. He just wanted contact. So, bit by bit, we were reassured. And the more he wanted contact with the outside world, the more certain we became that he hadn't passed the knowledge on, and the more determined we became that he was not to see or talk to a living soul outside of our carefully chosen jailers."

Gregory added, "And he didn't."

"Until Mr. Kendall," Windham said pointedly.

Kendall said slowly, "You don't think—"

"No." Windham was very emphatic. "Of course not. We wouldn't be here if we thought any such thing. But looking at it scientifically, as a statement of impersonal fact, it bears repeating: Hollister had no contact with the outside world until you visited him."

Kendall looked blankly at Windham's pompous face, which seemed to be trying to convey a subtle meaning beyond its powers of expression. But the restatement had only one meaning for Kendall. Scientifically stated or not, the implication seemed clear. Uncomfortably clear. "Look, Major, you absolve me on the one hand, and then pose a problem that has only one solution—my involvement. I—"

"I absolve you of intent, Mr. Kendall—only of intent. And on that subject I know whereof I speak. Have you ever wondered why you got the job of interviewing Hollister?"

Kendall smiled. "That's not very flattering of you, but frankly, I wondered very much. I am not in the top bracket of free-lance reporters. I think I'll be pretty good some day, but until this assignment I hadn't had much of a chance to make a name. Before the war I worked on a couple of small newspapers and then on the staff of a sizable monthly magazine. I did reporting for them—research articles. They liked me; I did fairly well. I think that if it had not been for the war I'd be well established by now, either on the staff of a magazine or paper, or even as a free-lancer. But as it is—" He paused, groped for the explanation. "I don't mean to imply that I'm any worse off than anyone else who saw service—but we're *all* in the same boat. I served just under four years, but you can almost multiply it by two when you come to evaluating it as a chunk out of my life. For a long time after I got back I rattled around aimlessly, telling myself I deserved a rest. And then when I started working, I started far behind the spot where I had left off. As a result I stand far behind the expectation that my age and possible ability would indicate in the line of work I've chosen. In fact, if I were editor of the *Courier* I'd have picked a dozen other men before me."

Windham said, "Eighteen."

"I beg your pardon?"

"Mr. Cressman, of the *Courier*, picked eighteen men before he came up with your name. He was very much annoyed by that time and he said—forgive me, Mr. Kendall—but he said you were desperation."

"I don't understand."

"Well, you see, we had been approached by many publications with requests for interviews, but we had turned them all down. By the time the *Courier* asked, however, we were on the pan. You see, you think we should have said to the press, and through them to the public, 'Hollister stole the secret of Seutaconawa and he wants to pass it on to the Russians. He is a traitor and we can't give you the details now, but we're going to be sure, in the interests of your protection, that he doesn't succeed.'"

Kendall said honestly, "Right. That's exactly what I've thought all along."

Windham said, "You must forgive me again—but you simply don't know what you're talking about. The protection of our secrets is not your business, after all, and you don't understand all the factors involved. One consideration among the many was that we didn't want the name of Seutaconawa on the front page of every newspaper for weeks at a time—"

"But everybody knows—"

"No, sir. That's where you fail in understanding our business. A few people in the East suspect. The handful of ranchers who live around Seutaconawa are curious. No one *knows* anything."

"I have heard"—Kendall was very positive about it—"a dozen people say that at Seutaconawa, Montana, the H-Bomb is being perfected."

"No doubt you have. But you are an Easterner, and a writer. The country at large has never heard of the place. If we had given that statement to the press, we would have found ourselves dealing with sight-seers." He added grimly, "—maybe with guided tours."

Kendall realized that it did make sense. But—"What about my eighteen predecessors?" he asked.

"Well"—Windham looked disgruntled by the memory—"by the time the *Courier* made its request we were in an untenable position." (Kendall remembered Hollister's gleeful comment: "I have become a *cause célèbre*, and they are stuck with me.") "So we decided to let the *Courier* do their article. But we insisted on passing first the author, and then the story. And we rejected the first eighteen names Cressman submitted."

"Good heaven!" Kendall stared at him.

Windham said hastily, "Oh, they were probably all right—probably all loyal Americans, but in each case we dug up something, *something*. And we weren't going to take the most infinitesimal chance. You were the nineteenth suggested interviewer. And may I say that the outline of your status that you've just given us is far less detailed than the one we could recite. We were—very thorough."

"Good heaven," Kendall repeated in an awed whisper. Then he started to laugh. "I always wondered why I got the job, and I knew it was a fluke of some kind, but I certainly never dreamed that my ability had as little to do with it as all that."

Gregory said quietly, "If I may be permitted to invade *your* field for a moment—may I say that I thought it a magnificent piece? With as little knowledge of the man as the time you spent with him permitted you, you still managed to capture all of him. Really magnificent. Also, it wasn't an entirely haphazard choice. Cressman explained that you had never done any big jobs, but that he thought you might do this one exceptionally well. According to him, he had been watching you because he thought you had an unusual flair for characterization. And, in my opinion, he sure was right."

Kendall felt fine. His head was up. He felt fine. He said, "Okay, thanks for telling me. But—where are we? Hollister was guilty. No civilian except me contacted him. You are willing to absolve me. My house has been raided. Where do we stand?"

X

Gregory smiled at Kendall. "Question to the point, as usual, Mr. Kendall. But from here on out I'd better leave it to the major. He has more answers than I."

Windham said pontifically, "It doesn't require answers. It's obvious. There is something in your series of articles that will tip the—uh—information. We have thought of trying to stop publication, but it would be almost insurmountably difficult. The *Courier* is very powerful, and they would fight it. Naturally. No magazine could look with dispassion or equanimity on so drastic an invasion of their editorial commitment to their readers. They are, however, a worth-while, intensely patriotic organization, so if they were told by the proper authorities that such a move was necessary they would certainly comply. But we have no open and shut proof, so that convincing the people who are in a position to enforce such a measure on the *Courier* would be insuperably difficult. Anyway, the second issue is already spread all over the country, ready for sale. We'd never get them all back. And the issue that holds the third piece is half off the press. Dozens of them are floating around the *Courier* building. There are even a few 'not-made-ready' copies—whatever that means—containing the fourth in the series in the production department of the *Courier*.

"No. The simpler, more feasible method is to find the message and delete it."

Kendall waited. Finally he said, "Yes?"

Windham's high color had receded and his anger seemed dissipated, but now he looked embarrassed. "But we *can't* find it," he said. "We've got the original manuscript back from the *Courier*. We've read it and reread it. We can't find anything."

"And you think I can?"

"We hope you can."

Kendall looked blank. How the hell would he know? He wouldn't even know what to look for.

Windham tried to answer his expression of bewilderment. "You see, Mr. Kendall, there's a time limit—that's why Hollister precipitated matters by committing suicide—and we know that date. Presumably Hollister's heirs don't know the date, but the conclusions of haste to be drawn from Hollister's suicide must be even clearer to them than it is to us, since they undoubtedly understand his character and motivations and reasoning better than we. So they know that he rushed publication, and therefore they know there's a time limit. The first installment apparently didn't help them, since they've started on a search for the rest of the material. If they—"

Kendall interrupted. "You mean the bomb is going to go off on a certain date?"

Windham looked disconcerted. "Something like that. Yes, you might put it that way. I've told Gregory that date, but that's all I've told him. I'll tell you that it's only a few weeks away. You see"—he paused and looked searchingly at the ceiling. Then he brought his gaze down and fastened it on Kendall. Kendall felt X-rayed. "It's impossible for me to make it clear. They need not merely the date, but the fact. It isn't just a matter of the explosion of a bomb. There's a secret, and in it lies our hope of eventual peace. Real peace. A peace that will go farther and deeper than uneasy armistices, than armed and wary zones of influence. We've lavished time and money and hope on our preparations. Once exposed, it would be utterly valueless."

"So what it comes down to is that you want me to see what I can uncover."

"That, Mr. Kendall, is it in a nutshell. Meanwhile, we shall try, too. And we will continue with our other precautions. We'll watch Miss Wentwirth carefully—"

Kendall felt a prickling sensation at the back of his neck. He arrested his first words before they could leave his mouth and reduced them to a two-word question: "Miss Wentwirth?"

Gregory turned his glance from Windham to Kendall. He looked curious. "Why, yes, Mr. Kendall," he said. "We feel about her somewhat the way you do."

"The way *I* do?"

Gregory said dryly, "I read your piece, Mr. Kendall."

"Ah—yes."

"If she hadn't said she barely knew Hollister, we would have absolved her completely. But since there was obviously no reason for him to lie, she must be lying."

Kendall should have felt vindicated and triumphant. He didn't.

Gregory said, "Whatever her knowledge, it's imperfect. Either she didn't understand what Hollister told her, or he didn't trust her enough to tell her anything at all, or —possibly—her involvement is of a different sort, an—uh—moral lapse. In the latter case, she lied to protect herself in another way and is probably entirely without implication in the affair. But we can't be sure. At any rate, although it was our first intention to hold her incommunicado, America just doesn't work that way. In view of the public uproar over Hollister, we didn't dare add coals to the bonfire. And it seems to have been just as well. Her telephone tap reveals nothing"—Gregory smiled his charming, small-boy smile—"except an interesting call from you, Mr. Kendall—and she hasn't contacted anyone. We'll just watch her carefully."

Windham hoisted himself out of his chair as if he weighed twice what he did. The mannerism was another facet of his character, Kendall decided. Just as Windham's stance suggested embonpoint that wasn't present, and his jutting jaw made him seem older, so his manner of handling himself suggested that he was a larger man than he actually was.

Windham said, "Gregory?"

And Gregory said, "Yes, Major, you're right. There's really nothing more to say."

He stood up, and Kendall followed suit.

Gregory added, "Thank you, Mr. Kendall. I think we've

accomplished what we came for. You believe in Hollister's guilt, and you appreciate the importance of the problem. You'll do your damndest to see if you can find a solution?"

Kendall said, "Certainly. I can recall the article almost line for line, and I'll go over and over it. If I find something—?"

Gregory gave him a telephone number, and Kendall wrote it down. "But," Gregory added, "we'll be in touch with you."

When the door had closed behind them, Kendall looked at the clock at the end of the hall. It was ten-thirty. They had been in his apartment for slightly over an hour and a quarter.

It seemed like a lifetime.

XI

Three hours had passed before Kendall permitted himself to realize that he was stalling. He had taken an unusually lengthy shower. Then he had tackled the straightening of the apartment. He had not been content with putting things back into a general kind of order, but had undertaken one by one the little improvements he had been putting off for a year—things like raising the mirror on the inside of the hall closet door and hanging the shelf he had bought for the bathroom over six months before. He did not merely replace the books—all several hundred of which had been dumped in the library corner of the living room—on their shelves, but found himself dusting each one and developing a precise rearrangement of their order. Books used for research on the lower shelves— But then he discovered that "research" was too general a word. He broke it down: language—foreign—bottom shelf, right. Above them he mentally designated, "English and grammar": Fowler, Thesaurus, Oxford, Webster, two English grammars he had never opened. Above that went religious books: an explanation of the Koran; a book on Jewish rites and their meanings; the Bible; a Hymnal; a Bible concordance.

When he tackled the biographies he couldn't decide

whether to break them down into periods or nationalities. If—

It was at that point that he stopped himself, stuck the rest of the books haphazardly on the shelves, and sat down on the couch.

Why was he stalling?

Communion with himself, the patient examination of his motives, was a hated but integral part of his existence. Some point of conscience insisted that he examine the why of his actions, and so Kendall always tried to understand himself. He succeeded admirably on the surface level, and failed completely in ever grasping any deeper motivation. He was dimly aware of the failure, powerless to change it, and made unhappy by his impotency.

It took him only a minute of self-examination to decide that he was occupying himself to avoid thought, and that the thought he was trying to escape was a wish to call Marta Wentwirth. His second, and completely erroneous conclusion, was that he was fighting the impulse because her wire was tapped and he had no desire to have his conversations open to the entire United States Government.

That satisfied him temporarily, and he was able to proceed to the business of recalling, almost paragraph by paragraph, *Genesis of Treason,* and the possibility of there being a code or meaning in the work that he had not intended to put there.

He went into his kitchen and fried some bacon and eggs, and while he ate his lunch, the book as it had appeared in manuscript form appeared before him, and behind it the factor that gave it its virility—the inescapable, vivid form of Francis Burton Hollister, alive, passionate, galvanic.

He tried to ignore Hollister and see only words. But the words, too, were Hollister's.

Hollister had been a quoter, and an extensive one. His quotations were cleverly chosen and strategically placed, and Kendall had taken full advantage of them. As it had worked out, that had required some small memory feats on Kendall's part.

When Kendall was finally permitted to see Hollister for the first time, he had been surprised by the extent of the precautions the Army exercised. He was taken first to a small barren office in which he was relieved of his belongings. His wallet, his loose change, his fountain pen; the watch off his wrist, the heavy platinum ring off his finger, the pencil out of his pocket; his cigarettes, his cigarette lighter (he had smoked Hollister's during the five visits) —every loose object had been politely removed. A corporal had typed a list of the articles in duplicate, initialed one, and handed it to Kendall. Kendall had then been escorted to and locked in with Hollister, and that list was the sole object on him, other than his basic clothing.

So he had had no opportunity to make notes.

After the first visit he had thought briefly of asking permission to take a pencil and some paper into the cell with him, but he had decided against it. Although once he had met the prisoner he found it hard to believe that anything on earth could make Hollister self-conscious, he still had ruled against taking the chance of inflicting on Hollister the stilted feeling that note-taking causes in some interviewees. Instead he had asked permission to make notes in the little office that he always returned to in order to pick up his belongings.

That permission had been readily granted and, after each visit, Kendall had stayed there while his memory was still fresh and made extensive notes before he left the building.

As he sat now in his little kitchen he realized again how much the story was Hollister's doing. Kendall deserved credit, and he didn't underestimate it. He had taken Hollister's words, and Hollister's quotes, and he had put them together with far greater strategy than had Hollister himself. Kendall had had to piece Hollister himself together, bit by bit, through what he had to say. And when it came to the writing of the biography, he had done that piecing for his readers. Using mainly Hollister's own words, he had arranged them to vast effect, and interpolated and interpreted exactly where necessary.

And still—*Genesis* was largely the words of Francis Burton Hollister. And his quotes.

Quotes. He kept coming back to the quotations. Hollister had, in his choice of reference, circled the earth and roamed boundlessly in time, rarely giving credit lines, except in his Bible references, and in that case he had the Book of Reference lying before him. But Kendall had recognized most of the quotations and had checked them in his Bartlett before he used them. So—

So Hollister hadn't used the device of misquoting.

Kendall stood up decisively. Nevertheless, the quotations were a definite possibility. In one way or another. He would tackle them systematically.

He installed himself at his living room desk, a very comfortable place at which to work because he had sawed off the legs of the massive old desk and so was able to lounge before it in a comparatively low armchair.

He started by making a note of the quotations in the order in which they occurred in the article. He didn't bother to write the longer ones out, but just made a reference that would be sufficiently clear to recall the whole to him. The list started off easily: "Old Chinese proverb—'Half an orange tastes as sweet as a whole one.' Jeremiah 36:22—'Now the king sat in the winterhouse in the ninth month, etc.' "—and so on down the sheet of paper. He had almost covered the paper before he realized that the order of the quotes could have no meaning since in writing the book he had rearranged them at will. Still the order in which he had employed them was the simplest way to recall them to memory.

At the bottom of the page he wrote: "Old saying (Southern?)—'A blind sow once found an acorn' "—and then sat back, startled by the appropriateness of the saying. He was the blind sow, all right. And he wasn't sure he would recognize the acorn even if he found it.

His low chair was on a level with his newly arranged

research shelves. Directly in front of him was the group devoted to religious research. His eyes ran absently over the neatly placed books—the Hymnal, the Bible, the Bible concordance . . .

His eyes snapped back to the sheet of paper before him. Of the nineteen quotations he had remembered so far, included were Chaucer, a song popular around the turn of the century, Liam O'Flaherty, Rabelais, and a couple of others—but the rest, ten of the nineteen, were Biblical.

And Hollister had named the article—*Genesis of Treason.*

A Bible? No—Marta's Bible.

Hollister had been trapped with his secret in Marta's apartment. He had known how little time he had—no one knew better than he how quickly the Army could move in the event of a possible breach of security. So where would he secrete a note? In Marta's apartment—a place likely to be the last in which he would have any freedom of action.

Suddenly an echo of Hollister's words came back to him. He had said something about starting his reminiscences with a story about a woman. . . . "The gods, to avenge themselves, sometimes grant us our desires. She was my desire, and the gods are avenged." And then he had said he was leaving her apartment when he was picked up, and had added a phrase, a vague, romantic phrase—or it had sounded romantic . . .

Kendall struggled with the memory. He squeezed his eyes shut and placed Hollister in his mind—against the wall, the sun falling warmly on his shoulders, the hair glinting . . .

". . . *Something of myself died there with her . . .*"

Ah! Kendall opened his eyes.

And then he had an unarguable reason for calling Marta.

He said, "Miss Wentwirth?" The quality of formality was as clearly present in his voice as in the words.

"Yes. Is this—" She paused. Then she changed the phrasing: "Who is this?"

In the pleasantness of the preceding evening they had, naturally and easily, progressed to the use of first names. He supposed she was a little bewildered by what seemed like a withdrawal on his part, but he couldn't make his voice any warmer. Upon him was the feeling of the ear at the keyhole, the human eye in the picture on the wall, the unseen wire attached to the typewriter, busily making a duplicate in a distant place. When the awareness of spying exists only in the mind of the watched one, the sensation is known as a type of insanity, and Kendall had a momentary glimpse of how terrible the experience must be. But at that minute the reality was as real as it could get—somewhere, perhaps a great distance from Marta's apartment, a recording was being made of his voice and hers. Their words—and more, their intonations and intimations—would be open to conjecture, to interpretation—

He said frigidly, on a rising note, as if she might not be able to identify the name, "Bob Kendall—?"

"Oh, yes—" She stopped, and then, avoiding any use of a name, "How are you?"

"Fine, thanks. And you?" This was silly; he had not thought beyond the moment of discovery, the feeling of revelation as his eye lit on the Bible, switched to his list, and gleamed at the memory of Hollister's title. He had not planned his conversation for two ears, and he now had a little feeling of panic that prohibited his use of common sense. He wished only to disguise his voice, his feelings, his question from the unseen listener. He said abruptly, "Are you free for dinner?"

If he had been inviting her to witness a hanging, he could not have been more abrupt or his tone less warm, and as she paused, he was tensely aware of how he had sounded. She would not see him, she would not—

When she said, "Yes. Thank you" in a voice as frigid as his, he found that his right hand was tightly clenched. He opened the hand and looked at the palm as he said, "It's almost three o'clock—"

"Not before six."

"I'll see you at six, then."

They didn't say good-by.

After he had hung up, Kendall examined his red palm. I must stop that nervous habit, he thought. And, with satisfaction, But they won't get to the Bible. *I* will. If there's anything there, I'll turn it over to them. It wouldn't have done simply to ask if she had a Bible. He could have asked, of course, but they would have rushed over . . .

The inexorable conscience arose and asked what difference that would have made? Why *not* simply ask her? Why *not* let them go over to her apartment and recover the Bible?

For an uncomfortable split second he was face to face with his underlying motivations, and then a flashing piece of logic spared him the unveiling: if Marta Wentwirth were involved, as it seemed so likely she was, here was the answer to why she had made no incriminating moves. She didn't know where to find the information. If he had mentioned the Bible she could have shaken the volume, fished out Hollister's notes, map, whatever the hell it was—and passed the information on. It fitted beautifully.

He couldn't possibly have avoided seeing her.

XII

Marta Wentwirth lived in an unpretentious building in the upper Eighties. Kendall knew from his previous visit that its individual apartments were pleasanter than the uncompromisingly bare graystone front would have led one to believe, and the rooms were larger and airier than its narrow, pillarlike exterior seemed to permit of.

When Kendall pushed the bell beside Marta's name, a returning buzz released the latch on the front door. He opened it and walked through the dim little lobby to the self-service elevator that was twenty years newer than the house and underlined the fact by seeming ridiculously modern.

But the elevator's snail-like pace belied its appearance. As it crawled toward the sixth of the building's seven stories, Kendall mused wryly on the living habits of New Yorkers; born New Yorkers, like himself, or the transplanted variety, like Marta—their habits are the same. They live in apartments variously described, with the fractions, as between "one-and-a-half" and "three-and-a-half" rooms. This is almost rigidly true of single New Yorkers, and it also applies to a large percentage of the married. When a couple has children they move to Queens, perhaps, if they are in the lower brackets; Stamford, Connecticut, is a typical transplanting ground of the upper middle class. It is surprising and amusing that the well-to-do—not the rich-rich, but those who are extremely comfortable—also reside in the one-and-a-half to three-and-a-half-room apartments—larger rooms, but no more of them.

The language, invented by landlords and now used like an incantation by landlords and tenants alike (and almost every Manhattanite falls into one category or the other), is a tightly ritualistic idiom that came into existence in the early thirties but became the standard means of communication with the arrival of the war years. A one-room apartment is impossible—a contradiction in terms—because the existence of a kitchen is what makes the residence an apartment. One-roomers are either hotel or rooming-house dwellers. But put a stove and an ice-box in the shallowest of closets and you have a kitchenette; that makes it a "one-and-a-half-room apartment." If you can get both feet in the nook that contains the stove and ice-box, *and* sit down in there, it is a kitchen. Kendall could get into his kitchen, but Marta couldn't squeeze into hers; therefore he had a three-room apartment, while she had only a two-and-a-half.

When she admitted him he found, however, that in the process of mixing cocktails she was doing the best she could to insert herself into the minute kitchenette.

He said, "Can I help?"

She laughed. It was the second time he had heard her laugh, and he warmed to the laugh just as he had that first time. It was a pleasant sound, more musical than her uninflected voice would have led one to expect, although it could not have been described as impulsive, or free and easy. She said, "Nice of you, but as matters stand I won't be able to get in here myself if I gain a pound."

He examined her hundred and ten pounds, wrapped in some kind of soft green silk, and commented that he thought that was an exaggeration.

His recognition that she became more attractive with each meeting gave way hastily to his desire to get into the living room and look at the books. It would have been a completely natural move on his part to have strolled in there, but with the usual perversity brought on by a guilty conscience—or, anyway, he corrected himself, an ulterior motive—he found himself unable to make the move.

He looked over her shoulder at the small window above the stove and said, "At least you have a window. My kitchen is large compared to this, but it has no ventilation. When I broil a steak the smoke backs into the rest of the place and makes like a London fog."

She said with the paradoxical, understated pride that the cubbyholers of Manhattan always evince, "This apartment has its drawbacks, but it also has a number of good points. Ventilation is one of them. I have four exposures."

"No!" His surprise and its implied admiration were real. Four exposures belong in houses, which are almost unheard of among middle-class New Yorkers.

"Well," she admitted, as she handed him his drink and poured one for herself, "No. Not really. I've got windows on four sides. The living room is south and west, and the bedroom is south. But this"—she gestured at the small kitchenette window—"and the bathroom face east, and the dressing room off my bedroom, north. The catch is that the bathroom, kitchenette, and dressing room look out, if you can call it that, on a narrow little air shaft. You've never seen the whole place, have you?"

He shook his head.

"Well, come along; I'll show you."

She led him past the bath, stopping in the doorway to indicate the window, and through her bedroom, which impressed him as being the pleasantest, airiest room he had seen in a long time, and from there into a neat little dressing room, banked with drawers and shoe shelves on the right, a long table against a mirrored wall on the left.

"There," she said.

He followed her gesture, passing her and looking out the small window at a total lack of view. The air shaft stretched about twelve feet in front of him and was only about three feet wide; all that was visible was graystone and the exterior of several of the small windows, each equipped with Florentine glass to prevent overneighborliness.

He turned back to her. "I still think it's wonderful. You certainly get cross ventilation, and a good deal of light, too."

"Yes, it does add light, but that's because I'm next to the top floor. The apartments below me must get progressively darker as you go down. I shudder to think what the ground floor must be like." She lifted her full glass to remind him of the one he was holding. "Let's go into the living room and drink these in comfort."

He followed her back through the bedroom, admiring the way it had attained femininity without having a frilly thing in it. He would have liked to comment on it, but he always found compliments difficult, even the most impersonal kind.

In the living room, he sat, sipping his drink, in a comfortable chair. At the far end was the single, not very large, built-in bookcase. As they talked, the bookcase loomed larger and larger until he felt that it had taken over the room, but he seemed unable to think of a way to get across the little space between him and it.

She finally gave him the opportunity. "More?" she asked, indicating his almost empty glass. "There's a little bonus—?"

"All right. Yes, thanks."

He surrendered his glass, and as soon as she was through the doorway he made for the bookcase. She kept up a light chatter from the kitchenette and he answered when it seemed necessary, but he had no idea of what either of them said.

Then, at his elbow, she said, "Here you are," and he leapt into mid-air in slapstick style.

"I'm sorry. I didn't mean to startle you."

As he looked down at her with an embarrassed smile, it seemed to him that her eyes were darker, her small features more rigid. My guilty conscience, he thought. He said, "Nice books."

Marta crossed the room to the chair she had vacated.

She took a considerable time in answering. When she did, it wasn't an illuminating remark. "Really?" she said.

Kendall, his eyes again glued to the book spines, said, "Uh-huh," before the quality of her voice and the inappropriateness of the remark got through to him. He pivoted slowly until he was facing her. She was sitting rigidly, her hands folded in her lap. She didn't look away, and now her eyes were definitely black.

"Have I said something?" he asked.

"No." Her stare was uncomfortably level. "No. It's what you haven't said."

"I don't follow that."

"Why don't you simply ask me where I keep my Bible, Mr. Kendall?"

He thought, It's no use. She's as guilty as hell—of something; I'm not quite sure what. But outside of that she's—out of range. What was the phrase she had used? "Not alive." Well, that was too strong, but she was certainly withdrawn. Between his helpless imprisonment in diffidence, and her inaccessibility—

He shied away from the completion of the thought and, his head thrust forward, his eyes barely visible, asked, "Where *do* you keep your Bible, Miss Wentwirth?"

She said frigidly, "Upstate. It was my great-grandmother's, and it's much too fragile to be carted from apartment to apartment. Satisfied?"

"No. Shall we go to dinner?"

In the silence that followed, his mind said, as it had

while he shared silence with her over the telephone that afternoon, She won't go; she won't go.

When she finally said, "Yes. I'll get my coat," he instinctively followed the pattern and looked down at his hand. This time, as the blood flowed back, his nail marks showed white on the red palm.

She reappeared in a coat of a soft-green color that was darker than but the exact tone of the dress. There was some fur of a pretty brown color at its neck, and it came to him that if she had not been good-looking she would still have caused heads to turn in response to the distinction of her clothing and carriage. But at that moment her face, too, was—breathtakingly arresting.

It's anger, Kendall thought. The anger gives her something of the vitality she lacks—the touch of abandonment. And then he noticed her hair—the black hair that supplied the frame for the heightened color of her face and the contrast to the soft-green color of her coat. The black hair was loose and soft and unfettered.

Uncharacteristically, but unquestioningly, he took the swaying hair as a personal tribute, and something inside him let go and was free. It was an electrifying sensation, almost of fulfillment—as if someone were pulling up a curtain, or rolling away a heavy weight. In just a minute he would be in the sun, or in the air, he would—

He drew back, or forward, or together. You do not dissolve in front of a stranger because you find her pretty, or because she's done you the compliment of wearing her hair in a fashion you once said you admired. You do not—

But he had a great wish to give her something, to offer something. He said, "I wanted to know about the Bible because—" And at exactly that moment she said, "I knew you were looking for a Bible because—"

They didn't laugh, but they smiled. He thought, She felt exactly as I did. She wanted to give me something, too, so she offered the same thing as I offered her—an explanation. And in response to her "Go on," he said, "No, you go on."

"Well, this afternoon just before you telephoned, Mr. Gregory—a Mr. Gregory of the FBI?—" He nodded. "He came to see me. There was another man with him, I don't remember his name, but I had seen him too when—before. It was the first time anyone had come or called about—it—since quite a while before the trial. They asked me if I had a Bible, and when I said no they came in here and looked, as if they thought I might be lying."

He said gently, "It was because they thought, as I thought, that Buddy Hollister might have secreted a message in your Bible."

"And you came to make sure?" Her aloofness was changed only by a little line that etched itself beside her full mouth, but he had learned to read the sign.

"To make sure—? Oh, I see what you must think. No, no. They didn't tell me what they thought, and I didn't know until you told me just now that they were here. We came to the supposition independently, but it's pretty easy for me to figure that out now, don't you see?"

She nodded, and the line beside her mouth disappeared.

XIII

He chose the best restaurant he could think of, and, as they settled at the table, he was pleased with his choice. The room was large but quiet, and the décor was simple—consisting, in fact, of little except an almost unending chain of exotic wine and whiskey bottles placed one touching the other along the top of the continuous banquette. There was no music, no loud voices, no feeling of haste or bustle, nothing but politeness and peace and the best food New York could offer. At the highest prices. But this was the first time he had tapped his new and considerable fund, and he found it a pleasant sensation.

They had settled against the divan and had given their order when Marta looked around the quiet room and said, "The people in here seem very much—alone."

"Alone?" His eyes traveled over the other diners. They were mostly in twos, although there was one large group. There wasn't a person sitting alone. They all, he thought in passing, seemed thoroughly bored. He looked questioningly at her.

"I mean—" She waved her hand in the helpless little gesture he was coming to recognize as despair in the face of an inability to express herself—"locked in. I mean—" She gave it up, and looked at him rather blankly. But he thought he saw a touch of a plea behind her expressionlessness.

"I see what you mean," he said slowly. "But why did you happen to mention it at just this moment?"

This time the blankness was genuine. "Because they *are*. These people"—she nodded at the tables—"*do* seem alone, without each other. Mentally, emotionally."

"But haven't you ever noticed that quality in people before?"

"Well, of course." Then she looked puzzled. "I suppose I have. Occasionally. But these seem more—more . . ." Her voice trailed off. "If they feel that way, people do something about it, I suppose. I've always supposed. So many of them here, though . . ."

"I see." He stared at the tablecloth.

She leaned forward. "*What* do you see?" The plea was there again, but when he looked up he forgot it in his reacquaintance with the line of her head and shoulders. She asked again, "What do you see?"

"Well, it would be presumptuous—?" His eyes asked permission and she gave it with a nod. He said, "Most people *are*—alone, as you put it. It is, I should say, the tragedy of—" He couldn't bring himself to say "life"; he substituted: "—everything. I think a few people overcome it, but they must be a very, very small minority. However, almost everyone *knows* it, feels the lack, and is powerless to fill it, close the void. I—" He hesitated, and then said firmly, "I feel it very keenly. But you— I may be wrong, of course—but it seems to me you've never even missed—

communication. And so you think it's merely a matter of choice."

She said slowly, "I see."

Conversation lapsed, but not uncomfortably, and when it started again, it dealt with small things, pleasant things, shared things. They had little on which to base a conversation since Hollister and everything connected with him would have been an unthinkable intrusion, and yet they managed to share the little that remained with a peaceful easiness.

But as they sat over coffee his usual state of embarrassment was brought forcibly back by Marta. She was guilty of the imposition, he decided, because the subject was new to her, and she did not recognize the meaning and discomfort it held for him. Like an unself-conscious child first told the details of sex, she wanted, in fascination, to pursue the subject. But he was like the embarrassed parent—old and twisted in knowledge, frustration, and remote connotations.

She reopened the conversation by asking, with what amounted in her to vivacity, "Communication—you know, about communication?"

He nodded, with a little smile. She seemed so unusually earnest.

"Well, what do you mean," she asked, " 'you feel the lack'?"

"Just that."

"And you can't do anything about it?"

"No."

"Do you try?"

He looked at her eager but puzzled face, and saw that she did not realize how very personal a question it was.

He said, "Look, this is beyond my depth. I suppose the answer is that I think I try, but something I am not aware of, or can't control, keeps me from trying hard enough." He paused, sought for an explanation, didn't find it. He added vaguely, "You have to kind of give."

She pondered that for a minute and then sat back with an air of decision. "Then all you need is an inner trust."

He smiled. She had certainly managed to reduce the problem almost to nonexistence. "I'm afraid it's not quite so simple as that."

"No," she said slowly, "I'm sure it's not. But it must be composed of things that add to that. As you just admitted by inference."

"Well—" His awkwardness was growing, and his little laugh was an embarrassed one. "Whether it's inside me, or outside me, whether it was caused by something in the past, or by fear of the future—it's me, now. There's no cure, I'm afraid. Or—" But he couldn't finish it. He couldn't plead with this young woman. He couldn't ask a stranger and a woman if she could fix his world for him, make him whole and happy. But he had got near enough it so that he was in a state of rigid discomfort. And added to his discomfort was the knowledge that he had a lingering, undismissible hope that in her next words would lie the answer.

"I suppose not," she agreed. "I suppose you are what you

are— But I should think if you could ever trust someone—completely—without reason—" She shrugged.

He felt cheated. It was an illogical reaction, but he couldn't help it. To be able to apply her cure you would first have to conquer the disease.

"Well," he said again. Then he laughed. "May I quote Hollister, as I seem to do increasingly often? 'If a man knew where he would fall, he would spread a blanket first.' I'm not quite sure what it means in this connection, but it sounds appropriate."

XIV

The next morning Kendall came wide awake without his usual drowsy interlude. His mind was crowded, churning, tumbling with unrelated facts and impressions. He lay quietly in bed, trying to compel his brain to take its cue from his relaxed body. But he still had the running-over sensation.

The FBI. The CIC. Smart. Quick. They had much more than he to attend to, but they had nevertheless wasted no time in beating him to the deduction about the Bible.

A false deduction? He and the authorities had both arrived at it. But where was the Bible? If she had known—

The "she" in that thought was more arresting to him than any conclusion to be drawn from guesses about the Bible. He started on another of the many seething thoughts. This one took the form of a kind of tabulation. One: she had gone to dinner although the invitation was, twice over, almost insultingly phrased. Two: she had seemed more alive, more concerned with the emotional aspects of living. Three: she had worn her hair—

He wrenched his mind from the ridiculous listing and tried to switch it back to the Bible, to *Genesis*. But the evening persisted in intruding itself. A strangely peaceful evening, a hiatus. Had he been guilty in permitting himself to be undermined? But he *hadn't* been undermined.

He had carefully and consciously refrained from any discussion of wire taps or followers—although, knowing of the detective's existence, he had not found it difficult, when an opportunity had arisen, to spot the man who had accompanied them to dinner and back to her apartment.

But negatively? Had he spent time with Marta—relaxed, peaceful time—when he should have been sweating over his memories of Hollister, his line-by-line recollection of *Genesis*?

And had she shown too little curiosity about the search for a Bible? Or was that merely a manifestation of her usual impassivity?

The doorbell rang.

As he walked down the hall, pulling on his robe, he called out, "Who is it?"

The pleasant, even-timbred, boyish voice said, "Gregory, Mr. Kendall."

Kendall opened the door. "You must eat Wheaties," he said sourly.

Gregory laughed. "Sorry." As he followed Kendall through the hall, he added, "You've been rather busy yourself, I see. Deducing, dining, and house cleaning."

Kendall chose only that part of the sentence he wished to acknowledge. "The maid dropped in in her unpredictable fashion someplace between six and ten last evening."

"She did a good job."

"Not only that—she doesn't even seem to have been surprised by the upset. She left a note—'Dear Mr. Kindal—

what a party!' Why do bachelors always get characters for maids?"

"I think it's the other way around. Maids, faced with bachelor clients, turn into characters."

Kendall said, "Maybe that's it." He hesitated on the living room threshold and then turned back. "You're going to have to perch on a hall chair, Gregory. There isn't room for both of us in the kitchen, and I want breakfast. Have some?"

"Just finished." Gregory settled on a chair in the hallway and watched Kendall through the kitchen door. "The note sounds as if she admired good parties."

"What? Oh, Lena. Yeah, doesn't it?"

"Maybe she thinks you don't throw enough of them."

Kendall slammed the coffee pot down on the stove, and swung around toward Gregory. He said forbiddingly, "What's on your mind this morning? My domestic problems, or my dinner companion?"

Gregory looked blandly undisturbed. "She's not in the clear, you know. Something damn fishy."

The rush of anger took Kendall by surprise. He said, "Now, look. I'll spare you most of the speech, but you've got one coming. About minding your own business, about considering people innocent until they're proved guilty, but most of all about psychoanalyzing me. My social life—how many parties I do or don't throw—is none of your damn business, Gregory. Leaping to the conclusion that Miss Wentwirth is going to sweep me off my feet because I'm—underamused—is one hell of a nerve. I—I—"

Gregory said loudly, and Kendall realized it was the third time he had said it, "Sorry!"

Kendall stared at him in suspended motion. Then he turned around and took eggs out of the refrigerator. He said, "What you don't seem to realize is that I have no part in all this. No real part. You want me to try to help—I'll try to help. But I don't owe you anything."

There was a little pause. Then Gregory said softly, "American, you know."

Kendall said violently, "Sure, I'm an American. I'm a New Yorker, too, and I don't like the subway mess, but I don't feel impelled to change my life to help clear it up."

"Not the same thing, you know."

Of course it wasn't the same thing. It had been a ridiculous remark. Of course he was involved. By birth, if nothing else. He said, "Okay. Maybe you'll feel better if I tell you that I went over to Marta Wentwirth's last night to look for a Bible. You had beaten me to it, but that was my reason."

"I do feel better. Glad to hear you've been working on it. Of course she had got rid of it."

Kendall spoke without premeditation. "She didn't have one."

"How do you know?" Gregory did not sound sarcastic, or even dubious. He was merely asking for information.

"I—" How did he know? And did he know? She looked pretty; she had worn her hair in a tumbled fashion. He didn't know anything. "I don't know. I mean she said she didn't have one."

He settled down at the cabinet to eat his breakfast, but he no longer felt hungry. He said tiredly, "But if we examine it coldly, it doesn't make sense to assume that she had and discarded a Bible. According to you, it doesn't make sense. If she had the information she would have turned it over. Or you would have caught her in the act of trying. So our Bible gambit was just a wrong guess, it would seem."

Gregory said thoughtfully. "I think you're right. Well, I only dropped around to see if you had come up with anything. You'll try again to see what you can dig out of your memory?"

Kendall nodded.

Gregory stood up. "Don't leave your breakfast." He stood still, involved in a thought. Then he said, "Might as well tell you. We expect Marta Wentwirth to try to skip. She's sat it out with a good deal of nerve so far, but from experience we know that when things begin to pop people start moving around."

Kendall lifted leaden eyes. "And what will you do?"

"Nothing. Follow her. Good if things stir up a little." Gregory said, "See you soon. Call me if you get anything." He moved down the hall, out of Kendall's line of vision.

As the door opened, Kendall called out, "Gregory!"

"Yeah?"

"*I* might as well tell *you*—I'll probably take her to dinner tonight."

There was a little silence. Then Gregory said, "Yeah? Well, good-by." The door closed.

The rest of Kendall's breakfast tasted better.

XV

The day was Thursday, Kendall realized—and, he told himself with a certain lack of clarity, the days do not wait. Wait for what? Wait for discovery, for personality, for growing up, for awakening. Or for espionage. In other words, he had things, everyday things, to attend to, including a date for lunch.

But he never kept that appointment. And he didn't even telephone to break it.

He had dressed and made a few phone calls, and was just sitting down to get in an hour's work before lunch on the puzzle of Hollister when the phone rang.

It was Gregory, and all the boyishness had gone from his voice. He said brittlely, "Kendall, can you come down here?"

"Come down where?"

"Oh. Sorry. I'm at the *Courier* offices."

"The *Courier* offices? What—? Well, I promised to get downtown for lunch in—"

"This is important."

"Well, if you really want me, I guess I can make it down there and still be in time for—"

"I want you." Gregory paused, and then added, as if he, too, had heard an echo of Windham in his voice, "I would appreciate it very much. This is—quite important."

"Well, of course then. It'll take me fifteen minutes."

"I'll meet you in the ninth-floor reception room." He disconnected.

Kendall stared at the receiver, and then shrugged.

The ninth-floor reception room was a newly familiar area for Kendall. Most of the editorial offices were on that floor, including that Mecca of top-flight authors, the office of Ben Cressman, the *Courier's* editor.

The receptionist recognized him and smiled. That in itself, Kendall thought, implied prestige on his part, and had almost a dollar value. She said softly, "The young man, Mr. Gregory, said you would be along, Mr. Kendall. He has temporarily taken over Mr. Mayer's office since Mr. Mayer is out of town. You know where it is, don't you?"

Mayer, the associate editor in charge of nonfiction, was Kendall's contact on the magazine. Kendall nodded and went through the inner door and to his right.

Gregory was alone in the paneled room, sitting behind a large clean desk, apparently doing nothing. He looked up as Kendall came in. He seemed abstracted and, Kendall thought, completely out of place. Desks and interiors did not become his redheaded vitality.

He said, "Kendall. Glad you came so quickly." Then he lapsed back into his abstraction. It was strangely out of character.

Kendall said, "Glad if I can help. What is it?"

"It's a new move. While it was by no means unpredictable, there is a peculiar angle. They—" He stood up. "Come along. I'll show you."

He strode out into the hall and turned left, and Kendall followed.

They moved down the long hall, away from the reception room, and into precincts Kendall had not seen before. At the far end of the hall Gregory turned left again and entered what should, architecturally speaking, have been a room, but which turned out to be a nest of halls. Kendall realized after a second that it had originally been a room, a large open area, but it had been turned into a maze of narrow lanes by the file cabinets that stretched upward almost to the ceiling and were rectangularly placed to take best advantage of the space available. The morgue, he judged. And the records. And the repository of dead manuscripts and old artwork. All efficiently kept in one area. Very different from the haphazard arrangement that had existed in the magazine he had worked on before the war.

The section they were in was devoted to narrow drawers, drawers that would accommodate nothing bigger than three-by-five file cards, but somewhere in here must be the original manuscripts of many great authors, and the original artwork of the men who had first raised magazine illustration to a fine art. Names flitted through his mind. Somewhere here—

Gregory took a sharp turn and Kendall, following on his heels, lost the fanciful trend of his thoughts. Because he had apparently arrived in the Valhalla he had been imagining, and it had none of the mouldering but consecrated air of peace he had romantically assigned to it.

Five young women were working with determination and understandable grimness. Around them, heaped on the floors, tumbling out of the large drawers, unclipped, unstapled, torn, twisted, and flung as if by a tornado, was more paper than Kendall had ever seen in one place. Eight-by-eleven sheets. Typewritten sheets. White sheets, yellow sheets, browning-at-the-edges sheets. Manuscript paper.

Kendall said, "Good God Almighty!" One of the girls shot him a glance of appreciation. He had apparently expressed her thought. He turned to Gregory. "When—Have you any idea—"

Gregory said, "Sometime after six-thirty last night and before eight-forty this morning. Which is not a very brilliant deduction, I'll admit. Let's go back to the office."

In Mayer's office Gregory resumed his seat behind the desk, and Kendall sank limply into a leather armchair. He said numbly, "They certainly have a real instinct for destruction, don't they? That havoc—that—that hysterical violence and chaos—it couldn't have been entirely necessary."

Gregory nodded. "Destructive people."

"How did they get in?" It wasn't an important point, Kendall thought; it was merely the first that occurred to him.

"Nothing very difficult about that. Magazines do not expect to be burglarized—what's the burglar to swipe? The ashtrays? However, there *is* a night watchman. One for the whole building—nine floors and a penthouse. He makes his rounds every two hours. Ambles through the building and punches a time clock on each floor. His real value lies in the fact that it would be difficult for a fire to gain any headway before he discovered it. He's a nice old man, and he's utterly bewildered by the whole thing. He saw nothing, heard nothing, knows nothing. And that's completely understandable. There are a dozen ways to gain entrance and, once inside, ducking him would be the easiest matter in the world. He doesn't go into the individual rooms, isn't required to.

"But it isn't really important how they got in. I'll have the place patroled in the future. It won't happen again."

"Isn't that precaution a little late?"

"Why, no. They didn't get what they were after, and God knows they're persistent. It's extremely likely that they'll try again."

"But you have the manuscript at your headquarters, don't you?"

"Yes, but this place is riddled with galleys of your damned reporting." Gregory smiled briefly and said, "Sorry, but that is currently my sentiment."

Kendall was too absorbed in the problem to respond to the smile. He looked thoughtful. "Of course there would be galleys. I hadn't thought of that."

"Well, they didn't find them. There's a strange paradox here." Gregory spoke slowly. "They looked in the wrong place; no current manuscripts or galleys are kept in that file room—aren't sent in there until a few months after the material has appeared in print. But—here's the paradox—they did have an idea of where to look in the sense that they went unerringly to 'the room in which manuscripts are kept.' No other office was disturbed."

"Well?" It seemed a small point to Kendall, and not particularly paradoxical.

"Well, my first reaction was that since they knew exactly where they were heading, probably someone who worked here tipped them off. But that's no good."

"Why not?"

"Because anyone who worked here would also know that your piece would not yet be consigned to the file room."

"Oh."

"The next logical assumption is that someone cased the building and came up with a fairly intelligent conclusion—that just happened to be wrong."

Kendall struggled after him. "Deduction is not my business, but that one seems to follow pretty neatly."

"So I looked for outsiders. That was foolish of me—You don't see that?" he added in response to Kendall's uncomprehending look. "Well, finding out who visited or snooped around this building in the last several days—or even weeks—is absolutely hopeless. Really out of the question. People come and go with every conceivable kind of reason. You can't even sift those who have a legitimate mission from those who don't seem to have. On the one hand you'll have someone who seems aimless and purposeless and who turns out to be honestly if misguidedly seeking the answer to 'how to get published.' And on the other hand you can have a guy who comes by appointment to discuss art, or promotion, or article ideas, or a thousand other facets of publishing—but whose purpose really is to case the joint." He shook his head. "Hopeless. It would mean the undivided attention of several men working for an indeterminate amount of time—and the result would most probably be absolutely nothing. The FBI is thorough, but it isn't foolish. Give us—oh, a laundry mark, for instance. We may have to check every laundry in the country, but that mark came from somewhere and our chances of reward are good. So we'll expend any amount of energy. But in this case—" He shook his head again.

"However, against both my common sense and my training I made a stab at it. And I came up with something odd almost immediately." He paused. "You know," he added musingly, "the element of luck never fails to astonish me. My estimate that it would take many trained men many days is a perfectly legitimate one, and yet I've only been here a couple of hours, and I'm lucky to have had that much time. Mr. Cressman is a smart man. The minute this was reported to him, at nine this morning, he called my office. When I left your place I reported in, and they gave me his message."

He lapsed into silence.

"So you came over here, and although you've only had a couple of hours you've come up with something odd," Kendall prodded.

"Yes." Gregory looked at him with a strange expression. "I had a stroke of luck. Seems pretty clear. That's why I asked you to come down here. See what you think." He abruptly picked up the phone and said, "Mr. Mayer's secretary, please. . . . Miss Ackerman, this is Gregory again. Will you give me another minute of your time in Mr. Mayer's office? Thanks."

He hung up and said musingly to Kendall, "I wonder if there is any business in the world that isn't occasionally disconcerting? You get everything all clear in your mind—you think—and then something fouls up the—"

The door opened and a pleasant-looking woman entered.

Gregory stood up. "Ah, Miss Ackerman. This is Mr. Kendall. Sorry to disturb you again, but will you sit down here"—he drew a chair up against the side of the desk so that she was facing both of them—"and tell Mr. Kendall about Mr. Mayer's visitor of yesterday? The visitor who wasn't scheduled. Sorry to ask you to go through it again."

Miss Ackerman sat down gingerly and said, "That's quite all right." But the expression on her plain face was one of slight bewilderment. "I don't know just what you want me to tell him. There wasn't anything—"

"Just describe her."

"Oh. Well, she was sent up by personnel. There isn't an opening, but she seemed unusually capable, especially of rewrite, and good rewrite people are hard to find. So they sent her up. She was here only a few minutes." Miss Ackerman looked lost.

Gregory prodded gently, "It's her physical description, mainly—"

"Oh, yes. Well, she was of medium height—one of those women who look taller than they are—and quite slender. Her hair was dark brown and slightly wavy. There wasn't anything about her features. I mean—they were all right; in fact, she was quite pretty, but her nose wasn't big or unusually small or—"

Kendall said furiously, "This is an unwarranted assumption on your part, Gregory. I think you have an unmitigated nerve. Did you bring me here to identify anyone from that vague description?" Miss Ackerman's flustered embarrassment penetrated his anger and he said to her, "Please excuse me, Miss—Uh. This girl was apparently average—average height, average coloring, average nose, average weight—there's no reason you should be able to give her distinguishing features if she didn't have any. But Mr. Gregory—" He stared coldly at Gregory—"Mr. Gregory, by the same token, shouldn't expect to make identification from such flimsy—"

Gregory said firmly, "Hold it, Kendall."

Kendall closed his mouth, and Gregory added, "Just a minute before you— Just a minute, please." He said to Miss Ackerman, "What about this girl's eyes?"

"Her eyes. Yes. Well, as I told you before, they're a little hard to describe. I *think* they were gray. But I'm not sure. They were—very pretty, and rather unusual. They—" She stopped, at a loss for adjectives.

"All right, Miss Ackerman." Gregory smiled at her and said in dismissal, "Thanks so much. I'll try not to bother you again."

As the woman reached the door, he called after her, "Just one more thing. You remembered her name—?"

"Her name was Mary Worthington."

The door closed behind her.

Kendall hadn't opened his mouth since Gregory shut it. Now he kept it closed and stared mutinously at Gregory.

Gregory said, "They can't find the application she filled out in the personnel department—the one that caused them to send her up here. She brought it up with her. Either Mayer stuck it somewhere—we called him long-distance but he can't remember what he did with it—or it simply got lost in the files, but in addition to the girl's name, Miss Ackerman remembers that she came from a small town in upstate New York and had worked there in advertising agencies. She said she had just arrived in Manhattan."

"Really?" Kendall asked politely. He stood up. He stared down at Gregory for a minute, and then turned and walked to the door. But at the doorway he stopped and turned back. "I thought Marta was being followed? How come you didn't know she was here—if she was?"

"Yesterday morning she lost her follower."

"You suggest it was deliberate? Because I'll tell you right now that she has no idea she is being trailed."

"You *can't* tell me that, Kendall. You don't *know* how much of an idea she has. And as to whether it was deliberate or not—" Gregory shrugged. "She left home during the morning rush hour, leapt into a subway kiosk—and that was that. We didn't pick her up until she arrived home in the early afternoon."

Kendall listened with stolid hostility. His only answer

was a question: "Tell me one thing—why did you bring me here?"

"Well—" Gregory looked compassionate, and a little tired—"I was disconcerted, and I wanted confirmation. We don't have much time, and you seemed to offer the possibility of a quick identification."

Kendall said coldly, "You won't get any confirmation out of me."

Gregory said gently, "I already got it, Kendall. Now I'll take some more—orthodox steps."

Kendall turned back to the door, but he didn't open it. He stood facing the paneled brown surface, studying the grain of the wood. He wasn't conscious of actual thought, but he had a feeling that something was wrong. Yes; one thing was wrong. He swung on his heel and said, "*Why* were you 'disconcerted'?"

Gregory looked up at him with a startled expression.

"Just a few hours ago you told me you expected her to skip. If you were that certain of her involvement, why should you be surprised if she turns out to be a—an advance man for them?"

Gregory looked upset, confused, and then—slowly—amused. "The laugh's on me, Kendall. I was—disconcerted—enough so that I mentioned my confusion to you. I forgot that you have the knack of asking good questions. And that one—from your point of view—is a damned good question. The only trouble is, I'm not going to answer it." He stood up. "Look, why don't you go home and—"

Kendall closed the door on the rest of the sentence.

XVI

He didn't like drugstore lunches, and he wasn't quite sure how he had arrived at this counter. But he had, and he had also ordered a sandwich, since it was now being placed before him.

He started to eat it.

There were things to think about, he felt. If he could make his mind a blank—if he could eat with attention—he would not have to think.

But the habits of the mind are not so easily broken. Kendall was in the habit of trying to think things through. This matter did not bear thinking about, but he couldn't sweep it away. In the middle of a sip of coffee, realization, accompanied by a sudden nausea, swept over him.

He downed the nausea, but the realization clung and spread. Marta had gone to the offices of the *Courier* the day before. She had spent hours with him during the evening, and had not mentioned the fact of her visit. And last night, perhaps shortly after she left him, the offices of the *Courier* were searched.

Now, wait— He stopped the tumbling thoughts.

There was no reason to assume that she had been on the raiding party. In fact, it was most unlikely.

But what was the difference?

And why *should* she tell him that she had gone to the

Courier—for some reason of her own? He was a stranger. She hadn't told him every detail of her day's activities; in fact, she hadn't mentioned one thing she had done, and why should she have?

But it was no good.

Kendall left the wrecked, half-eaten sandwich, and the drugstore. When they called after him, he returned to collect and pay his check, but he never knew that he had neglected to tip the fountain man.

He walked home. It was thirty blocks, but he barely noticed them.

So Marta was guilty. Of what? "Undefined crimes," she had said, was what he had accused her of. It was an apt term for his present state of mind. He had no idea of what she had done, was doing, or her reason for it.

Suppose they had something on her—suppose it was a kind of blackmail? Suppose—

Gregory had suggested, on that first visit to his apartment, that Marta may have been involved in some way without being in the least concerned in Hollister's act of treason. "A moral lapse," he had said. If someone knew of that and was putting pressure on her— But he flinched away from the explanation. It didn't seem to put matters in a much better light.

He walked and he thought, and he got nowhere, but as he entered his apartment, he made an astonishing discovery. The nausea was gone. The pain was gone. It didn't matter what she had done. It simply didn't matter. Blackmailed or not. Culpable or not. Marta was Marta, and in some way that was quite enough. Perhaps he would ask her—tonight. If he didn't think it would upset her. By that time, Gregory would undoubtedly have asked her many things.

And if Gregory hadn't got around to her yet, would he be justified in tipping her off, in telling her that her movements were known? Well, he would weigh his loyalty to what Gregory stood for against his loyalty to—to Marta, to himself, to his trust—

Her voice came back to him like an echo: "All you need is an inner trust."

He glanced at the living room clock. It wasn't three o'clock yet. Before he took off his overcoat he went to the telephone. Then he had to drag out the heavy telephone book, and he thought, I must memorize that number.

He said, "Marta?"

She said, and it didn't seem an odd answer to him, "Yes, yes, yes."

Then they didn't say anything for a minute or two, and the pause didn't seem odd, either.

He broke it: "Will you have dinner with me?"

"Yes. But why don't we have it here?"

"I'd like that."

"Good. I'll go out and get some stuff."

"Six?"

"Before, if you can."

"See you, then."

Not until he had hung up did he remember the silent

listener, the intruder who hung speechlessly on their words. His obliviousness amused rather than annoyed him.

He decided that Gregory hadn't been near her yet. Otherwise she couldn't have sounded so—blithe, so happy.

He smiled and settled at his desk—the Bible, the concordance, the Bartlett, pencils and paper in front of him—with a sense of calmness. This was important. This he could tackle and perhaps solve. The other—the other you left to trust, and six o'clock.

Two hours later his enthusiasm had dimmed considerably.

He had made a master list, which included every quotation Hollister had delivered himself of. With that list before him he had tried every trick of code, conundrum, or confusion he had ever heard of or could himself devise.

They all meant nothing to him.

One fact stood out: no matter how he attacked the words, from what angle he examined them, the Biblical quotations seemed the more important, more deliberate. The others were too dispersed. They didn't have an era, a nationality, a name, or an object in common.

He sighed wearily. Sometimes the expensive way was the best, the most saving in the long run. He would have to expend time. As Hollister had said, "Sometimes the man who goes to bed to save his candle, begets twins."

He started another list, abstracting the Biblical quotes from the mass.

Then he looked tiredly at it. Hollister had said, for instance, "The Army thinks I am a viper come out of the heat and fastened on their hand. So they are prepared to shake me off into the fire. Well, perhaps I am a viper, but have they forgotten that Paul wasn't hurt, didn't fall down dead when the viper bit his hand? Perhaps all I do is for the best, designed primarily to help them." Yes, that one was clearly from the Acts, the parable of Paul among the Barbarians. Hollister had twisted its meaning, but that was its source.

That was the only reference to St. Paul, but—Kendall got a little tingling sensation at the base of his neck—the other quotes were all from three books of the Old Testament—Jeremiah, Ezekiel, Daniel. And in each case, the quotations were bunched in a small section. Even if the bunching weren't significant, it shortened Kendall's job.

He settled back in the chair and started with Jeremiah. The quotes all came from the middle section, and started with the first Biblical comment Hollister had made to Kendall: "Now the king sat in the winterhouse in the ninth month; and there was a fire on the hearth burning before him . . ." and it continued through the story of the burning of a roll on which, at Jeremiah's instructions, Baruch had written the words of the Lord.

Kendall read through it twice and then said to himself, "Yeah?" and moved on to Ezekiel.

The quotations in Ezekiel came from the beginning of its fifth chapter. ". . . Thou shalt burn with fire a third part in the midst of the city. . . . Then take of them again and cast them into the midst of the fire and burn them in the fire; for thereof shall a fire come forth into all the house of Israel."

Kendall felt far more bewildered than he had over the naughty king in Jeremiah. He went on to Daniel.

Hollister had quoted extensively and tellingly from Daniel, particularly from—Kendall turned the pages—Chapters 3 and 4. These chapters contained the allegory, familiar to Kendall as it is to most people, of Nebuchadnezzar and his mistreatment of Shadrach, Meshach, and Abed-nego. Nevertheless, he read it again, enjoying the rolling phrases and the successful use of repetition. The story pyramided—Nebuchadnezzar got into a fury because Shadrach, Meshach, and Abed-nego refused to worship his golden image; he gave them a second chance; they still refused; he ordered them "to be cast into the midst of a burning fiery furnace"; they defied him again; he ordered that the furnace be heated "one seven times more than it was wont to be heated." Then—

Kendall was interrupted by the thought that Hollister had certainly chosen a bloodthirsty group of tales. Or, at least, fire-thirsty . . .

His head came slowly up from the Bible, and he stared into space. *"Fire." "Burn." "Hearth." "Burning." "Burn." "Fire."* And *"burning fiery furnace."*

Sure.

He read back. Every Biblical quote had something to do with heat and fire, hearths and burning.

He couldn't sit still any longer; he got up and started to pace the floor.

Marta's apartment? His original reasons for deciding that was Hollister's choice of a hiding place still held good. Marta's apartment was certainly the logical place. The stove, perhaps? It seemed unlikely. He tried to picture the place, but excitement had wiped his mind clear. He could see the general layout, and the pleasant bedroom came clearly to his mind, but the living room had a blank spot. The chair he had sat in dominated one corner; the bookcase was against the opposite wall; the couch was on the left—but what was opposite the couch? He drew a blank, but—it *could* be a fireplace; it was an outside wall.

He didn't need the telephone book; he had the number in mind now. As he dialed he realized that the call was unnecessary. It was now—he looked down at his watch—almost five-twenty. He would be over there in a few minutes, anyway. But he wanted to talk to her—he wanted to know if there was a fireplace in that living room.

He gave up after the telephone had buzzed six times. She had said she was going out to buy food for their dinner, but he would have thought she'd be back by now. However, by the time he got there she would probably have returned.

In spite of his growing excitement and his sense of urgency, he paused to burn his notes. He felt theatrical and a trifle silly as he watched them go up in flames, but just the same . . .

XVII

Kendall reached Marta's apartment house at twenty of six. His impatience had pyramided to such a point that he discovered, in the creeping elevator, that he was breathing shallowly and rapidly. He took a deep gulp of air and forced himself to a surface composure. By the time he rang the bell, he had himself pretty well in hand.

He felt slightly incredulous when his second ring brought no response. A tenant with a key had unlocked the main door just as Kendall entered the vestibule, so he hadn't used the downstairs bell. He had not felt it necessary to announce himself because, after all, he was expected.

He was expected. Why wasn't she there?

He rode down again in the infuriatingly slow elevator and then stood indecisively on the steps in front of the building. Wait for her? No. He thought it over, and then walked toward the avenue at his right. There was a corner drugstore across the side street, and he went in there and into the first of the bank of telephone booths.

He had intended to call Gregory, but instead he found himself dialing Marta's number again. Perhaps her doorbell didn't work. The trouble with that wistful thought was that he had heard the bell from the hallway, faint but unmistakable. Still—

But the phone rang with a distant, phlegmatic insistence, and he let it ring a long while before he put the receiver slowly back on the hook.

After a minute of staring at the bottle-green wall, he took out the slip of paper on which he had made a note of Gregory's number. Would Gregory be there so late in the afternoon?

Gregory was there, and Kendall was put through to him with surprising dispatch. But after Gregory had said "Hello?" Kendall found himself at a loss. What did he want? What could he—

"Hello!"

"This is Kendall, Bob Kendall."

"Yes. Hello. What's on your mind?" Gregory's voice indicated that he had snapped back to normal. The weariness and confusion of the morning were gone, and he sounded normally boyish and buoyant. He said, "You departed so—er—abruptly this morning that I didn't get a chance to apologize. I *am* sorry. I think it was unnecessary to put you through that—that trip downtown. What can I do for you? Or"—a note of eagerness caused Gregory's voice to retrogress until it sounded as if he were on the trail of a new part for his hot rod—"have you got something for me on *Genesis*?"

"No. It's just that— Miss Wentwirth isn't home." The inanity of the comment echoed in the booth.

"Isn't—?" There was a pause. Gregory said with amused interest, "Really?"

Kendall felt himself growing warm. "That sounds—

Well, you see, we had an appointment. She *should* be home."

"I see." Kendall heard the growing amusement, and suddenly knew that his face was red. The fact that he was all alone in a booth with no one to see the blush somehow made it worse.

Gregory said soothingly, "I wouldn't worry, Kendall. I talked with her around three-thirty. She was quite all right then. Any number of innocent things may have happened. Traffic at this hour– Look, we've got a man on her, you know. He's due to call in at six. That's"—there was a pause during which Gregory apparently looked at a clock—"that's only eight minutes from now. Why don't you give me a ring in ten or fifteen minutes?"

Bitterly, Kendall said, "Have you any assurance the man hasn't lost her again?"

Gregory said gently, "Now, Kendall."

"Okay, okay. I'll call you."

"Sure, do that. I'll hear from you in about fifteen minutes, then." The phone clicked off.

Kendall went back up the quiet side street. It was full night now, bitterly cold and achingly dry. The street seemed deserted, and the traffic sounds of Manhattan at rush hour had an offstage quality; the horns, squeals, rumbles, and whistles were unceasingly audible, but muted, in the wings. Automobile parking was forbidden before six o'clock, and very few drivers had jumped the gun. There were, at least at that moment, no moving vehicles. There were no pedestrians. Lights were all around him, but they all seemed dimmed—lamp-shaded, curtain-veiled, blinded, slatted, diffused. There was something about the lights that reminded Kendall of lights seen from a train at night—distant, unreal, inhospitable, twinkling remotely for people you've never seen, will never know, living lives you can't imagine, between walls you'll never pass.

As he stepped off the curb someone near him flicked a cigarette lighter. The little click and the ensuing glow startled him. He looked back over his shoulder just as the man standing in the doorway behind him lifted the flame to his face.

That was all; the man lit his cigarette and Kendall continued across the street, but the little incident had the effect of canceling out Kendall's feeling of isolation. He had been indulging in a picture of himself walking through a make-believe Manhattan—lit and rumbling, but actually deserted. A foolish far-fetched fancy, neatly blasted by the actuality—in Manhattan there is always someone at your elbow.

He mounted the opposite curb, crossed the sidewalk, and entered the small vestibule, where he touched Marta's bell. There was no answer, nor did he expect one. After a minute, during which he was not conscious of having a single thought, he chose a fourth-floor number and pressed its bell. Another hazard of New York life, he thought, and mentally apologized to the woman who left her dinner preparations, to the man who hoisted himself out of his easy chair—

The door's lock buzzed invitingly, and he went through the door and back to the elevator.

As he rode up to the sixth floor, he realized that something extraneous was bothering him. He couldn't put his finger on it, and his persistent, self-analytical habit forbade its abrupt dismissal. He was worried about Marta . . . but that was pretty silly. . . . Gregory was right—traffic was brutal at this hour. . . . He would call back in a few minutes, and Gregory would have the answer for him— His wandering thoughts drew up short. The puzzling, distracting point seemed to be right there. . . . But it slipped away again.

The elevator stopped at six, and Kendall got off. Then he stood aimlessly on the landing. There wasn't much point in pressing her bell, but he did so anyway. There was no answer.

The house around him seemed very quiet, and the hall was bitterly cold and surprisingly drafty. He shivered, turned up his coat collar, and looked around for the source of the draft. On the stairway, an unenclosed, winding affair that rose beside the elevator, he could see two windows—one a few steps above him, one almost a flight below him. The window above him was open at the bottom, wide open.

He mounted the few steps, his eyes on the window, and noticed that its panes were of Florentine glass. It must be —he looked out—yes, it led onto the slotlike air shaft. He stood on the stairs, his hands resting on the dusty windowsill, his head through the opening, and looked down into the shaft.

It was peculiarly lit; he could not think of anything he had ever seen that had quite that luminescent quality. It was dark—his first impression was that it was pitch black—but then he realized he could see fairly clearly. So there was light coming from somewhere. The light came, however, not from above, where the moonless night made it seem as if a black canvas had been drawn over the roof, but through a scattered few of the Florentine windows lining the walls on three sides. It was cold, so the windows were all closed; it was comparatively early, so many people had not yet returned home from their business day and only a few of the panes had light behind them; and the glass weirdly diffused what light there was.

But they weren't *all* closed. The window immediately opposite him was open a couple of inches from the bottom. That must be Marta's dressing room window, he thought.

And it wasn't dark in there. That is— He stared. It *was* dark. Completely so. His eyes were playing tricks. He had thought he glimpsed light, a flickering light—

And then his mind, diverted from the details of the air shaft by the direct connection of the word "light," leaped to the earlier problem that had been teasing at its fringes as he rode up in the elevator. The man across the street—the man who had outlined his face with the flickering flame of a cigarette lighter—he was Marta's watchdog. Kendall had had only a single glimpse of the man's face on the previous evening, but that glimpse had photographed itself in his memory.

They had come out on Third Avenue after dinner and found that cabs were hard to come by. It was the after-theater hour, and Marta had stood shivering in the doorway while Kendall and the doorman whistled and hailed. Kendall had finally spotted a cab crossing diagonally under the el, reversed his field, and dashed across to it. In doing so he passed within touching distance of the man who was leaning against a support under the far side of the elevated. Something about the man—his pose, the cold, the anxiety in the man's face—caught Kendall's attention and afforded him some wry amusement. Kendall knew all at once that this was the follower, that he wasn't sure he was going to be able to get a cab, that he was miserably cold, and that Kendall's unexpected maneuver had caught him unawares, and had given Kendall too close a look for the man's comfort.

Well, he had just got another look: the man downstairs at that moment was the same man.

Kendall leaned on the windowsill, shivering, his head thrust out into the black night. What kind of hours do they work? he wondered. And then, *What is he doing out there?*

He drew his head in and sat down on the stairs, and the shaking increased. He was very cold, or was it the cold? Pull your thoughts together, he told himself. Think it out. The man was across the street, so Marta was in her apartment. Was that open and shut? Could she have slipped out—evaded the man across the street? No; there was no rear entrance; the cellar exit was on the street, a precipitous cement stairway a few feet from the front door. Besides, the FBI wasn't staffed by fools; they intended to keep track of Marta, so if there was any other way out of the building they would have discovered it weeks before. So—

The ratiocination was foolish; he *knew* Marta was in there. Something had told him so all along.

Get the building's superintendent? The futility of trying to convince a superintendent that Kendall had a right to be admitted by passkey overwhelmed him. No.

He stood up. He would go back and call Gregory.

But—he stood indecisively on the stairs—what would he say to Gregory? "If your man hasn't called yet he will in a few minutes. He'll tell you Marta is in her apartment. And I guess she is—but she won't answer the door." He could hear in anticipation Gregory's controlled amusement as he explained that perhaps Marta was a heavy sleeper, that perhaps—"sorry, Kendall"—she had regretted her invitation.

No, he couldn't subject himself to Gregory's probable amusement and probable do-nothing attitude.

There was another possible explanation of the complete silence from Marta's rooms. Perhaps she had found the "fire" or "hearth" or whatever was hidden in that apartment. Perhaps she simply didn't want Kendall in the way.

No. No. That wasn't a possibility. He didn't know why; he wasn't going to bother to think it out. He was going to dismiss his eternal probing and accept on sheer faith that it just wasn't possible. At three o'clock that afternoon he had embraced trust; he would not let it desert him now.

Kendall reached up to close the window to the air shaft, and then stood with his hands on the sash, arrested in mid-motion, staring at the window across from him. He tried to collect his thoughts. I'm not seeing things clearly, he thought. I'm jumbled. A few minutes ago I noticed something at that window, or inside. Whatever I saw reminded me of the man across the street. Was it a light, then? Like the man's? A cigarette lighter, or a match? No—it had another quality. Also flickering, but—

The light came again, and then Kendall knew what it was. That abrupt sweep of light was more than a flicker—it glowed bluely and rapidly across the pane and then went out.

A flashlight.

Kendall closed the window and stared at the translucent floral pattern for another ten seconds. Then he moved decisively up the stairs. The man across the street *might* be accounted for; the flashlight could not be. It was the final proof. *Someone was in there; someone was in there with Marta.* And she wasn't answering the phone. And there were no other lights. . . .

Kendall crossed the seventh-floor landing and climbed the last flight, which led to the roof. The door to the roof opened easily.

XVIII

It had been cold enough on the street, but it was unbelievably icy on the windswept roof. Kendall moved cautiously around in the frigid darkness until his sense of direction led him to the air shaft. One side of the shaft was blocked off by the wall of the building next door, which rose a few stories above him. The other three sides had a brick wall around them—only waist high, just enough to keep careless strangers from falling in accidentally.

He drew his overcoat collar high around his neck, braced himself against the wind and looked over the wall, down the narrow slit. The weird faint light came up at him, and after a minute he could pick out the general outlines of the shaft.

It was hopeless. Any idea he had had of going down that steep hole was doomed almost before it had taken form. There wasn't anything in the shaft but gray stone and windows. No fire escape, no drain pipe, no obtrusion of any kind. At its bottom—he leaned over farther; not quite at the bottom—was a netlike, sievelike layer of wire, probably placed there to catch any débris that might be thrown out of the windows. And it seemed to have caught quite a bit of stuff; he couldn't distinguish the forms in the darkness—probably tin cans and such.

The wire looked like the nets they sling under aerialists. . . .

But he wasn't an aerialist.

And in reality it only *looked* like the nets they use in circuses. It wouldn't give if one fell on it; it would be far more—destructive—than a hard surface. It would chop into the faller. . . .

Kendall leaned to the right. There was Marta's dressing room window, invitingly raised from the bottom.

He hoisted himself up on the short end of the brick wall and sat with his back pushed against the side of the building next door. His feet then stuck out into space, about ten or twelve inches beyond the point at which the brick safety wall made its right-angle turn. His estimate of the width of the air shaft had been correct; it was probably a little less than three feet wide. If he were to rest his back against the wall of the building next door, his feet would brace him against the other side of the shaft.

Maybe.

He dismissed that irresolute amendment. He really had no choice in the matter, so he might as well focus on the practical aspects of the problem. The word "practical" struck him as being somewhat ironical, but he didn't pause to give it further thought.

The first question was, overcoat, or no overcoat? He finally took it off—unwillingly, like a man discarding a heavy robe to step into an icy bed. The result was even more penetrating than he had bargained for. He instantly began to shake so violently that he found it difficult to control his knees as he bent them and placed his feet flat against the wall a few inches down the shaft. Then he edged his body sideways and downward, out into space.

After a few minutes the cold gave way to a purgatory of heat-and-cold. I'll go to a gym, Kendall swore to himself. If I ever get out of here— But I'll never get out of here. I can't go down any farther, and the one thing in this world I can never do is go up. The incredible strain caused a constant sweat, and the shaft provided an updraft that bathed him in a steady, freezing current. Two or three times in every minute he sweated and dried.

He kept stubbornly inching downward. Drop my right foot two inches; brace my back; drop left foot. Then lower my hands two inches. What were his hands doing braced against the rough brick wall behind and below him? Nothing but bleeding—they were totally useless in the descent, but he was incapable of placing them in his lap, or of allowing them to dangle in space. A man is accustomed to helping himself along with his hands, and the fact that he was pointlessly tearing them to pieces seemed beyond his control.

His first rest and encouragement came when he reached the seventh-floor window above Marta's dressing room. His torn hands found something to hold to and he was able to draw his shoulders forward for a minute. The small window was ornately decorated on the exterior—over it a rounded projection, and under it a fancy extension of the interior sill. He wondered why the architects had gone to such seemingly insane lengths—insane in view of the fact that no one could see the exterior of the windows. No one except human flies. He giggled, and the giggle and the fact that, without exercise, he was in danger of freezing, seemed wrong to him. He thought, "Upward and onward." He noticed that he had said the words aloud. Then he corrected them : "Downward and inward."

The second giggle and the renewed strain aroused him to a small grasp on reality. But he couldn't stop himself from solving the pointless problem he had set: The architects, he decided, had planned and watched the house go up before the more modern building next door was erected. The drafty hell he was in had not always been enclosed on four sides.

He was not fully conscious during the last minute or two. The inching motion had become second nature, something he did to keep alive, and herculean effort though it was, it was better than remaining still in the freezing current that bathed him like a swift arctic river. So he moved automatically downward, and for a second, when his hipbone hit it, did not recognize the rounded protrusion that was the top of Marta's window.

He came more alert then, and instinctively cautious. He intended to enter silently, although he had forgotten why. But there were two terrible minutes: one when, as he swung his feet to the sill, his stiff, lacerated hands slipped off the top of the window and he had started backward, outward, before he got another, last-minute grip; and a second when he realized that he might not be able to get through the small window.

He managed it. The window slid up noiselessly, and he went in feet first. His shoulders caught, but he tugged and pushed and finally stood in the partial darkness of the little room.

XIX

Kendall did not know, afterward, how long he stood, motionless and almost without thought, in the darkness. He closed the window after him and turned around so that he was facing the open doorway to the bedroom. He was certain that he would never be warm again, but some instinct told him to wait and give the warmth of the room a chance. His knees, released from the terrible straining effort that had been demanded of them, shook uncontrollably. That, too, he felt, would pass. He leaned back against the window wall. He would just stand there, safe in the darkness, comfortable in the growing warmness, and his legs would become legs again, and his hands would stop hurting, and the blood in his veins would reach up to some reasonable temperature and start flowing.

And so he stood, without thought, vegetating in a womb-like fashion in warmth, and peace, and silence—

But it wasn't silent.

Unwillingly, strugglingly, his mind was forced to function. There was a sound, a number of sounds. Someone was talking, whispering, muttering. The sounds were very low, but once he had awakened to them, they became increasingly noticeable. Not one voice, at least two. Men's voices? He thought so, but he couldn't distinguish much tone, or any syllables. There was another sound, too. A rattling, rustling noise.

The shutters in his eyes had adjusted themselves to their environment, and the darkness had taken on form and shape, dark areas against darker masses. Ahead of him he could see the frame of the doorway, and then the bedside table beyond it. The bedroom held a little light, a very faint glow. That light, he realized, was coming through the hallway from the direction of the living room. Ahead of him, beyond the little night table, was the bed. And on the bed was—something. A coat? A few pillows? He didn't think so.

He moved, and found that his legs, wavering and uncertain, did, nevertheless, function. There was thick carpeting beneath him, and his progress was reassuringly quiet. Six steps took him to the bed, but before he reached it he could see its surface.

Marta was lying on the bed.

Her eyes were open and, as they stared strainingly up into his, full of messages. He could almost understand the tumbling thoughts behind the panic-stricken eyes. But her lower face was covered by the excess folds of a large gag. The folds made the gag—a pillowcase, he later discovered—seem like a soft, billowy mass, but then he saw the parallel indentations along Marta's cheeks: the gag was viciously tight.

Her arms were behind her, awkwardly so, and as he put his hands gently under her head to get at the knot of the gag, he noticed her feet—crossed at the slender ankles and tied together; the cord—even in that tense moment, he saw the little plated gadget that hung from her ankles and recognized the control cord from the venetian blinds—the cord went round and round her ankles and then off the edge of the bed and around its right front leg.

Her hands were beneath her, he realized then, because they, too, were bound together.

His own hands, bleeding, mutilated, painful to the point of agony, fumbled endlessly with the thick knots at the back of Marta's neck. And when he finally got the gag off, she still seemed unable to speak. Her full lips, normally so firm and contained, were bruised and swollen, and then he saw her tongue—dry, thick, seeming too big to be contained by her sore mouth.

He put a pillow under her head and turned her gently on her side, away from him, so he could get to her hands. As he worked on the strong cords—even more difficult to manage than the gag had been—he put his lips directly to her ear. He let the barest breath escape behind the syllables; he couldn't have been heard at a distance of three feet. "Don't even try to talk. It will be a while before you can enunciate, and you might make more of a sound than you intend. Just nod or shake your head. Except for these cords, are you all right?"

It was no time to notice it, but as he watched her head go slowly up and down the line of her cheek seemed lovelier than ever.

In his relief at her answer a little whistle of air escaped

him, and the two of them froze into complete immobility. But the faint rustles and murmurs from the next room seemed unchanged. The people in there were being almost as cautious as he was; they were probably no more than fifteen or twenty feet away, figuring the distance directly through the wall—perhaps thirty feet if one were to walk it via the hallway—but the sounds were very slight.

"How many are there?" he breathed. Then he realized that the question demanded a verbal answer. "Two?" he ventured.

Marta's head shook.

"Three?"

The head went up and down affirmatively.

Her hands were finally free, and he pulled her gently onto her back and laid the inert hands across her waist. "As soon as the feeling comes back, try to rub them, Marta. It'll hurt, but try."

He moved—cautiously, cautiously, not a rustle must escape the room—to the foot of the bed, and knelt there while he forced his outraged hands to work on the knots at Marta's ankles.

Three men. Might as well be a hundred. They probably had weapons of some kind, but even if they were three little men armed with feathers, he didn't think he had a chance. His hands were causing him agony; his whole body had the enervated feeling of muscle turned to water; the descent of the air shaft would take hours to overcome.

As he worked at Marta's bonds, insane little plans floated through his mind. He would station himself behind the bedroom door, entice the three men into the room by making a noise, and then hit them from the rear as they came through the door. Oh, yeah? his mind said back to him. And who is to guarantee that they will rush through in a Mack Sennett single file and fall in a neat pile? Well, then—he would go out the front door and get help. Passing the living room doorway by making himself invisible? Suppose he hid in the dressing room— In the shoe racks?

The last knot gave and he chafed the slender ankles briskly until it came to him that he was probably doing more harm to his hands than good to Marta's ankles.

He moved up to the head of the bed and, still kneeling at the bed's side, pulled her toward him and into his arms. Her eyes, enormous in the darkness of the room, seemed less panicky and, as he lowered his head to her ear, she give him a tremulous but reassuring smile.

He whispered, "Okay?"

Her head nodded against his shoulder.

He cradled her tightly. "Have they been here long?"

The head went up and down.

"What are they looking for? Do you know?"

He recognized the shaking of her body for what it foretold before the hysterical little giggle broke out. He had experienced the same panicky laughter in the shaft, and armed with the new-found knowledge, he put his hand gently but firmly over her bruised mouth. When her eyes had calmed, he took his hand away.

There was still laughter in her eyes, but of a saner kind,

and she mouthed the words thickly but without sound: "Bible fanciers, too."

"I see. Listen, Marta. I'll have to go for help. I can't take you with me so I'm going to put you under the bed. It's so obvious a place that maybe they won't think of it right away."

"How will you get out?"

He hesitated. Then he said firmly, "Up the air shaft."

Her eyes widened. "That's impossible!"

He silently agreed with her, but he didn't admit it. "I came down that way."

Marta digested that. It was obvious that she had given his means of entrance no previous thought. He was there, and she didn't care if he had dropped through the ceiling, but now fear for him came down on her. "Just the same—"

He saw the growing protest in her eyes and, as he moved her carefully off the bed and lowered her to the floor, he said, "See if you can help me, Marta."

As he had hoped, she responded to the plea without recognizing it as a partly diversionary tactic.

She whispered thickly, "Bob, we'll have to hurry. They come in and look at me every now and then."

Of course. The flashlight. Well, they would hurry.

But it wasn't so easy.

The big double bed was modern, which meant that it was very low to the floor. Getting beneath it presented a problem he had not foreseen. But the lowness would form an additional protection—no one would be able to see beneath unless he knelt and put his forehead to the floor.

With a good deal of squirming, sliding, twisting, and maneuvering, Kendall got her under the bed, but he wasn't satisfied until she had the added safety of being under its direct center. By the time they had managed that, he, too, was squeezed under the low frame.

There, he thought. A lousy hiding place, but all that—

The shot came from the wrong direction. No one can hit us from the end of the hallway, he thought. Why don't they come in here?

Then they did come in.

The blasting of the silence was more shocking than any of the fears or confusions that would follow it. One minute there were five people in a small apartment, and there wasn't a decibel of sound among the five. And then there was noise thudding at them—loud, incoherent, panicked, rushing noise. Voices, sentences, shouts. Running, pounding of heels.

Three feet came into view, inches from his nose. A voice right above him said in an hysterical, almost feminine scream, "She's gone!" Another, deeper voice, said with an effort at command and calmness that was in some way funny, "Of course, you fool. Where did you think they came from? She went for them." A squeak: "But how?" Another voice: "What the hell's the difference now? Help me hold this door. Don't stand in front of it! Are you crazy!"

Still another voice, from the hall: "Open that door! We'll shoot through it!"

A whisper: ". . . There *wasn't* any service entrance. Anyway, we're locked in *here*."

"I warn you! Stand back—we're going to shoot!"

The whispers multiplied: "Sheer drop." "Air shaft." "—Can't tell them we have her, you fool! *They* have her!"

Another shot—very, very close.

Kendall lost track, because Marta had begun to shake. His head was turned toward the bed's edge, away from her, and the bed's lowness made it impossible for him to turn around. His inability to help her infuriated him. Only his left arm could reach her, and he tried to gather her in with that, and couldn't do it. He knew dimly that there were many more men in the room, and the shouts and confusion grew louder and light flooded in on the periphery of his vision, but he had withdrawn his attention. One thought obsessed him: if he could crook his elbow just a fraction more he could hold Marta tightly, reassuringly.

He kept trying.

It was minutes later before his own name coming out of the hubbub engaged Kendall's attention: "What do you mean, they aren't here? Maybe she's not, but I think she is. And Kendall's certainly here someplace. Maybe he's dead, but then there's a body. For God's sake, Schwartz, look around. Try the closets—"

Kendall said, "Gregory. Under the bed."

There was a startled second of dead silence, and then Gregory's voice—calmer and with the slight undertone of amusement Kendall had come to know and dread: "Hello! Well, you can come on out now."

"That's not so easy. We're wedged. Will you lift the bed at the foot?"

The bed sailed upward as if it were a toy. Light poured over them. Kendall half closed his eyes against it and peered at the three men who were squatting in front of him. Then he ignored them.

He struggled awkwardly, stiffly, to a half-sitting position, so that he could turn. He said, "Marta? Marta?" And to Gregory—the middle of the three faces—"Well? Get a doctor!"

Marta's face, lost in the masses of dark hair, was a bloodless little triangle, frighteningly white, deathly still, entirely without sensibility.

XX

He felt better after the doctor had come and gone. The doctor said brusquely that humans lived on oxygen. "If you remove it," he added succinctly, "they faint. Keep it removed, they die. That girl in there was gagged?"

Kendall nodded.

"Yes." The doctor seemed remotely pleased that his diagnosis had been correct. "That's why her throat is constricted and breathing is abnormally difficult for her. Then she got jammed under a low bed— What miracles do you expect of a respiratory tract?"

Kendall felt criminal. "But she'll be all right?"

"A night's sleep. Fine tomorrow. Keep the windows wide in there." He waved toward the bedroom.

"Shouldn't we have a nurse?"

"Nurse wouldn't have anything to do. The girl's had a sedative. She'll be a little confused and upset when she wakes up. Just see to it that someone's around to reassure her."

"I'll be here."

The doctor eyed him sardonically. "And will she find that fact reassuring?"

Gregory answered for him, and Kendall could have kicked him for the little touch of amusement in his voice. Gregory said, "Infinitely, doctor. Infinitely."

The doctor said, "Um. Now, you. Let me see those hands you're holding as if they were someone else's. Let me see them!"

Kendall, feeling very much as the family doctor had made him feel when he was ten, held out his hands.

When Gregory said, "My God!" with absolutely no amusement in his voice, Kendall looked down. He had been postponing the inspection because he had a suspicion—but they were even worse than he had supposed. Not beef, he thought. Not chopped meat. Veal. That was it. The same deep pink color, the same soft look.

When the doctor left, Kendall's arms ended in two large white extremities. It had been a painful business, involving stitches, caustic disinfectants, and finally, before the vast bandages, a soothing paste. Also, protestingly, Kendall had swallowed some pills.

When they had all gone—all except Gregory—Kendall sat in Marta's living room and looked across the débris at Gregory. He waved at the books heaped between them, most of them slit up their spines, and said, "Looks like my place, doesn't it?"

Gregory pointed wordlessly at the coffee table, its mosaic-tile top pried off.

Kendall said, "I never set eyes on more than their feet —and only three feet, at that. Were they the same men who visited me?"

"Presumably. Probably made the night foray on the *Courier*, too. The same ratlike destructiveness. One is a known, important Communist agent; one is a handsome, well-dressed pig in a poke; one's a punk. Presumably the punk was in on the deal because he's pretty good at housebreaking. I'll give odds he did the professional job on your door. Identical method of entry here, and this place has a more intricate lock.

"They knew she was being followed, so they simply waited until she was out and had drawn her watchdogs off with her. Then they got in, but she came back and surprised them. I think maybe I should have anticipated their move and watched the house." He shrugged. "Hindsight, though. Easy enough to know what you should have done afterward."

Kendall looked down at his bandaged hands. "Feel a little silly about being under the bed. I was trying—"

"You came down the air shaft, didn't you?"

"Well, yes, but—"

Gregory said with an air of finality, "Well, I wouldn't have done that. I don't think I would have thought of it, and if I had thought of it I wouldn't have tried it, and if by some insanity I had tried it I wouldn't have made it." He added, "Besides, the bed was an inspiration. If they had known she was in there, they would have tried to use her as a hostage to assure their escape. They wouldn't have got away with it, but hostages often come off badly."

Kendall felt better. "How did you happen to come?" he asked.

Gregory stared at him. "You don't give us much credit, do you? I told you my man would call in. He phoned from a booth in the front of a lobby across the street. He could keep an eye on this house through the window. He told me you had gone up twice and hadn't come down the second time. I sent him up to see if you were waiting on the landing. You weren't. So, obviously, you had felt it necessary to get into the place. We just followed it through."

"Um." Kendall didn't think it was quite as simple as that, but he didn't know how to phrase his objections. "But you haven't always been quite as—clear-thinking, you know."

"No? In what way did we fail?"

"Well, it's patently obvious now that whether she was at the *Courier* offices or not Marta was telling the truth throughout, and Hollister was lying."

"It's been obvious all along. Until this morning, that is. And that's why this morning's incident threw me for such a loop. I had Miss Wentwirth neatly positioned in her slot of innocent bystander, and then she showed up at the *Courier*." He shook his head in unhappy reminiscence. "I began to think we had the whole thing pegged wrong."

Kendall felt anger welling in his throat. He said tightly, "And what changed your mind back again?"

"She did. I asked her if she was there, and if so, what she was doing there. And she told me the obvious truth with obvious honesty. She was annoyed at being tracked down and embarrassed by the fact that she had been discovered using a false name, but her explanation was utterly simple and patently truthful: She was looking for a job. She doesn't want to go back to her agency—feels they don't want her." He shot Kendall an embarrassed glance and hurried on: "So she went on a job search. Said she was bored with advertising agencies, and thought her qualifications fitted her for editorial work.

"After my man lost her at that subway—and, incidentally, I agree with you on that: she didn't have any idea she was being followed and it was simply the rush-hour mess that caused him to lose her. Anyway, after he lost her, she canvassed all the large magazines, left applications, and hoped for the best. I believed her, as I say, but to be on the safe side I had it checked up on. She was in almost every magazine office in the city that day. As for the fake-name business—well, she is understandably afraid that she'll be identified.

"But until the business of this morning—to which I momentarily gave too much weight—it was clear that she was and always had been innocent of any guilty connection with the affair. We had been watching her in the hope that they would try to get to her. Hollister's reasoning was pretty clear. His higher-ups knew he didn't have any contact to speak of with the Wentwirth girl; they knew he was picked up here. He was simply calling attention to her by a lie they would recognize for just that. So they knew they had to look here—but first they wanted to know where to look or what to look for. They caught on to the Bible thing, I guess, and didn't dare wait any longer for something more definite."

Kendall held his growing anger in a tight grip and tried

to speak calmly, "Her—truthfulness—wasn't obvious to me."

Gregory shrugged. "You were prejudiced and consequently blinded."

"Prejudiced?"

"Sure. 'Never trust a woman.'"

"I didn't say that."

Gregory shrugged again.

"Anyway, if you were so sure she was innocent, why did you lie to me? Why tell me she was implicated?"

"We didn't exactly. We just went along. That was how you felt, clearly revealed by the first of your articles. It was easier to let you go on under that impression. We—"

"*Why?*"

Gregory's boyishness receded. "Take it easy, Mr. Kendall. Our prime concern was to keep the information from reaching the wrong hands. Conversation, speculation, two people mulling it over, amateurs perhaps enlisting other amateurs—not good. We thought we could use your help, and so we asked for it. But when you showed an—ambivalence—in your attitude toward Miss Wentwirth, it was better to maintain that status than to have the two of you actively coöperating on a matter we simply don't want discussed."

Kendall said violently, "I think it was rotten. This morning, even before you had that little ghost of a reason for wondering about her, you went so far as to tell me she might run away."

"I was trying to keep you from getting in the way—

from some quixotic gesture like that descent of the air shaft."

"It's a damn good thing you didn't succeed, isn't it?"

Gregory's voice was gentler: "For Miss Wentwirth, yes. For us, not very much difference."

Kendall stared at him through a furious mist. "And how do you arrive at that conclusion?"

"After they got into this apartment, they were doomed. We would have caught them as they came out. There's the man across the street, and a man stationed at the corner; if you go across the roofs you exit at that corner. There was no other way out, and two of them would have been recognized instantly. Miss Wentwirth might– Something might have happened to Miss Wentwirth, but– Well, it's a hard thing to say, Kendall, and you are not going to forgive me, but her life is a tiny, tiny consideration in all this. We're happy, delighted, thankful to God that she is okay, and we're glad, since it turned out all right, that we didn't succeed in diverting you, but it simply wasn't a significant part of our worry. It was more direct, intelligent, important, from our viewpoint, to let matters pretty much alone, and just wait."

Kendall's fury had reached a dangerous stage. He stared down at his bandaged hands and said to himself, Hold on. Hold on! He managed a strangled sentence: "Well, you didn't get your information. You didn't find whatever Hollister hid, and I'm glad. I hope you never–I hope–" The strangulation closed his throat.

Gregory sounded very calm by contrast. "I'm sorry

you're so upset. You are not going to believe me now, but I know exactly how you feel. Maybe you'll realize that later. As for the 'information'—the people concerned in our Government *know* what it is, Mr. Kendall. We only wanted to grab it to forestall them, so that it wouldn't be around to fall into enemy hands. But now—well, despite their persistence it's finally become unlikely that they'll try again. We've caught one of the most important Communists in America, and we can put him behind bars, which we weren't able to do previously. We've also got another very important-looking prospect. And the time is running out. In a month or so, it won't matter if they find and *publish* the information; we will have succeeded. Or at least, that's how I understand it. We'd certainly like to have it; we'd feel safer. But this isn't too disappointing a dénouement."

He stood up. "I'll be going along. Windham and I will be around in the morning. Hope Miss Wentwirth has a good night. And if I were you I'd stretch out on that couch and try to get some rest." He walked to the door, but on the threshold he turned around and looked calmly into Kendall's glaring eyes. He seemed to consider, and then he said deliberately, "You're probably in no mood to recognize it, Kendall, but we've done you a favor. You did come to trust a woman—completely—and in defiance of a good deal of evidence to the contrary. It's a very valuable asset to happiness, you know. Or you'll find out."

He walked down the hall, and then the front door closed with a decisive little click.

XXI

Kendall came awake all at once, with no transition period. His watch said twelve. He put it to his ear: no tick.

It was still dark out. The lamps, the one at his elbow and the one on the table across the room next to the big armchair Gregory had sat in, were still throwing soft pools of light to the widened circumference of their shades.

Gregory. He remembered the click of the door as it closed behind Gregory, and then nothing.

He sat up. Although he had slept in a half-sitting position, he felt refreshed, and there were no cricks in his neck or his knees. The couch was soft and comfortable, and he had apparently relaxed into a restful, unstrained position. But his mangled hands hurt—burned, itched, ached, pained.

He hiked himself out of the deep couch without using his hands for leverage and tiptoed across the inlaid tile of the hall floor into the dark bedroom. He stood quietly and patiently in the cold blackness until his eyes grew accustomed to the lack of light, and then he moved across to the bed.

Marta lay as she had when the doctor left her; she didn't look as if she had moved since. She was on top of the counterpane, lying on her back with her head turned slightly in his direction and her chin lowered toward her shoulder. The extra blankets they had found, neatly cased, on a shelf in the dressing room, were still tucked around her. The loose white fluff that formed the collar of her dress was foaming softly around her face. It made a surprisingly clear accent in the dark room, and Kendall found himself trying to gauge the color of her face as against the pure white of the collar. A foolish attempt, but she did seem to look pretty good, and her breath came softly and evenly.

She looked infinitely sweet.

He turned and moved silently toward the door, passing the dresser en route. On top of the dresser a neat little electric clock whirred gently. Six-fifteen. He moved out of the cold room and drew the door to a crack behind him.

He went back into the living room and perched on the edge of the couch. He felt full of energy, full of a feeling of things to be done, but he was uncertain of where to start—uncertain, really, of what the matters were toward which he was so strongly impelled.

Well, there were the books. He would have liked to clear up the place before Marta awoke. No one knew better than he after his recent experience how depressing a ransacked house could be, and Marta's was normally so neat. But his hands—he looked down—the doctor must have put in his bandaging apprenticeship on a moving-picture lot. They looked like a close-up shot of a fat Invisible Man. He looked helplessly at the books and beyond them to the opposite wall.

And then he remembered.

He had been rushing over to Marta's the previous evening to look for a fireplace in the wall opposite the couch, the spot his memory had refused to furnish. Well, there was no fireplace. The wall was covered by a built-in unit, a handsome affair that included a television set, a radio, a desk flap, some pieces of pottery and glass. No fireplace.

What had been his second thought? Ah, yes—a stove.

He rose, stepped over the books, and tiptoed through the hall to the tiny kitchenette.

But one look was enough. Concealment in that neat little kitchenette—concealment of anything—was out of the question. Certainly not in that stove.

Rather aimlessly, he opened the little refrigerator, and was abruptly touched to the point of a welling feeling in his throat. There was his dinner—various kinds of lettuce, torn apart and washed, bulging in a fishnet sort of container. Beside it was an avocado. Through the glass partition at the top of the box he could see, neatly wrapped in transparent paper, a handsome steak. There was fruit and wrapped cheese on the bottom shelf. The intruders must have hidden in the apartment for some time, hoping she would go out again. During that time she had done the preparing. But if she hadn't gone out in the first place for the wherewithal for his dinner—

It was a far-fetched self-accusation, and he dismissed it.

He made coffee—Marta would need plenty after her sedative—poured himself a cup, and went back to the living room.

The coffee was hot and good. It was surprising, he

thought, that he had not felt the cold during the night, that it was as warm in the room as it was at that moment, considering the early hour. The bedroom was cold, but the window in there was wide open. Here, in the living room, only one of the three windows was down from the top, and then only an inch or so. Still, the apartment must be heated by city steam, or continuous hot water. Very unusual in these old buildings. His own place was frigid by midnight.

Heat. Warmth. "*Fire. Burn. Hearth. Fiery burning furnace.*"

He got up and threaded his way through the books to the pair of windows in the south wall. Below them was a window seat, running the length of the narrow end of the room. Imbedded in its top in four places were the interstices of a grill. It obviously doubled as a radiator cover. Beneath it was at least one, perhaps two, radiators. It was winter, and cold. Marta might turn her bedroom radiator on and off, but she would naturally leave the living room radiator on constantly in such weather.

He couldn't at first figure out how one got beneath the cover. Then he found the openings, two of them, on the perpendicular front of the seats. They were small doors, hinged on the inside, neatly fitted and very inconspicuous. It wasn't easy, because of the awkwardness of his bandaged hands, but he managed to open the right-hand one; it was lined with sheet steel and beneath the steel was asbestos, which showed between the nails that held asbestos and steel firmly to the door. Inside the dark opening were the expected coils of the radiator and the knob with which it could be turned on and off. It was dusty in there; in spite of Marta's obviously excellent housekeeping, the interior of a Manhattan window seat would be impossible to keep clean.

He closed the little door and moved to the other end of the window seat, where he knew what he would find. Yes; there were the final coils and the valve end of the radiator. He closed that little door and then stood looking out the window.

Well, it had been a thought. It certainly was the hot spot of the room. If Hollister had wanted to hide something, it would have been a logical place. Hollister could have figured out just as easily as he that Marta would not be doing much turning-off of the heat until the weather grew warmer. In fact, if it wasn't too far-fetched of him to presume that he could read Hollister's mind, that connection might have led him to the fire-hearth-heat-furnace clue. But Kendall thought, it *was* far-fetched, and anyway, all those references to heat and fire and burning in the Bible selections might have been coincidence.

But he didn't believe that.

Well, Gregory didn't seem to place much value on the finding of the message, the note, the whatever. So why should Kendall? But although he felt he ought, in defense of Marta, to remain angry, he couldn't seem to recapture his fury of the previous evening. One did one's job, and if your job was America, he supposed you had to weigh the costs. One girl's life against—what? An H-Bomb? An

Army? A hundred and sixty million people? Perhaps even the world? He couldn't know, and not knowing, he couldn't judge. They didn't feel about Marta as he did. She had become, he knew, without any sensation of surprise or sudden awakening, his reason for living. She hadn't replaced anything; there had been nothing to replace. And for that reason she was a million fold dear. Where there had been a noticeable, never forgotten void, there was now Marta.

Also, he had a sudden conviction that if Marta had meant all that to Gregory—yes, and certainly to Windham—they might still have chosen the course they did. An anger-defeating realization.

He stared out the window over the low roofs of the residential section in which Marta lived. Far off to his left there was a glow in the sky. A dusty, off-pink glow. The sun was coming up, but like every other thing in New York, it was forced to do its work behind a dust-screen that took its pureness of coloration from it. It might, and often did, achieve an unusually beautiful effect as it forced its way through the dust clouds, but it would almost never have the shine, the brightness, the *cleanliness* of a country sunrise. Nothing . . .

But the asbestos. The asbestos lining the right side of the radiator door showed at the edges of the steel as a dirty brown-gray; in the left-hand recess, part of it was a bright-white.

Even brand-new asbestos is not bright-white.

He thought he would never get the slip of paper from

between the steel insulation and the asbestos to which it was nailed. His bandaged hand had been too clumsy to hold the percolator when he had poured his coffee; he had finally, and with great difficulty, managed by using both hands. How could he expect to extract a slip of paper wedged between nailed-together surfaces?

He accomplished it in the end with a sharp grapefruit knife from Marta's kitchen. He held the knife with both hands, muttered, swore, and sweated. The paper came out an inch; it slipped back a half inch. He got it out, eventually, by kneeling and using his teeth.

XXII

The words were written perpendicularly down the slip of paper, which was about an inch-and-a-half wide and eight or nine inches long. They said:

American
Chin
Knees
Wil.
In Phil.
(T) rate
Chemulpo-Weihaiwei
Taitogai-Huithow Pt.
In
Doctor
Nation
Seutaconawa
Land
3/4
Approx. 2,000

At some point in his frenzied puzzling over the words Kendall stopped for breath, more coffee, and time to wonder why he was taxing his brain. The kitchen clock said eight-thirty. So he had been struggling with the list for well over an hour. It was difficult to hold a pencil, and he was no nearer a meaning than he had been when he first extracted the paper. The whole thing was none of his business; indeed, Windham would probably prefer that he not disentangle the message. And, anyway, he despaired of ever making sense of it.

So far he had decided only that it was a strange combination of geography and anatomy. Nine of the words, or lines, seemed geographical in sense—Seutaconawa was obvious, and the sight of it had given him a tingling sensation; "Phil." could be Philadelphia; "Wil." could be Wilmington—although that seemed a wild and baseless guess. The four Oriental words were presumably Chinese, Manchurian, or Korean. Perhaps place names. They seemed vaguely familiar. He had also thrown "Land" and "Nation" in with the geographical group, although it strained the category somewhat, but he couldn't bring himself to consider the adjective "American" as a geographical designation.

And what the hell were the anatomical references all about? "Chin," "Knees," and—roughly, roughly—"Doctor"? He had discarded the fractional aspects of the "3/4" and decided, in view of all the discussions about a date that Gregory and Windham had launched into, that it was a date. So something was going to take place on March fourth. But what was "(T) rate"? An Army tech sergeant?

The "Approx. 2,000" irritated him more than all the rest of the words put together. It was so clear as far as it went, but it so clearly needed a noun after it. Approximately two thousand *what?*

He lifted and balanced his cup of coffee and returned to the built-in secretary-desk in the living room. Every word on the paper was engraved on his brain by that time, but nevertheless he stared blankly at the sheet for another hour.

When the downstairs buzzer sounded, he rushed around the apartment in a frenzy, trying to locate the release button for the downstairs door before the would-be entrant got impatient and pushed the buzzer again. He wanted Marta to sleep as long as possible.

He finally found the little button-and-phone connection tucked away behind the kitchenette door. Then he stood absent-mindedly in the hall while he waited for the elevator to make its slow ascent, and his mind returned persistently to the puzzle.

He realized, and found the realization infuriating, that Hollister must have devised and scrawled the little list in a frantic hurry—without any preparation whatever. By all reports, Hollister had been in the apartment less than a half hour; he could have been alone in the living room for only a few minutes. Kendall's mind went back to the evening two days before when he had taken Marta to dinner. She had gone to get her coat and had returned in a very brief time. Presumably she had done the same with Hollister. She had probably made him a cocktail—perhaps he had written the message while she was preparing the drink in the kitchenette. Then when she went for her coat, he secreted it.

The reconstruction partially satisfied Kendall. He stood

absently in the hallway, thinking it through, and found one thing wrong with it: Hollister must have known where he was going to put the paper before he wrote it because he must have deliberately chosen to write in perpendicular fashion so that he would have a strip narrow enough to fit between the fairly close nails. It was obvious to him that he might be picked up before he got a chance to pass his information on, so he had left a message. That was straightforward thinking on Hollister's part, but the further implication was that the message could have had no preparation. True, Hollister was involved in the business of coding and decoding, but still . . .

The doorbell rang, and Kendall moved toward the apartment's door, still thinking. Hollister had written the words downward because of the space problem, and he had no time to think up an intricate code. And, as Kendall put his hand on the doorknob, those two facts, taken together, unraveled the code. It unreeled before his eyes with perfect intelligence, clear and concise. How could he have wasted so much time? . . . He opened the door and disclosed Gregory and Windham.

They were standing side by side in exactly the same position as that in which he had first seen them—on a threshold, hats in hand, expressions noncommittal as far as their characters permitted (Windham's would-be expressionlessness was tinged with pompous belligerence; Gregory's with deprecatory boyishness). His elation over the success of unraveling the message, plus his recognition of the distinctive quality of the two men's poses combined to amuse him. Kendall laughed.

They again reacted characteristically. Windham looked huffy; he apparently could conceive of nothing in the situation or in their appearance that could possibly evoke laughter. Gregory, on the other hand, looked amused and curious. He looked as if he wanted the joke explained so he could join in the laughter.

He said, "Just high spirits? Or are we naturally funny-looking?"

Kendall slowed down to a smile. "You looked—characteristic."

The three men walked down the hall, and he realized as he led them that they were imitating his tiptoeing. They really do mean well, he thought. When they can afford it.

As they stepped over the books, Gregory's quick mind caught up with the laughter. "Characteristic pose, and characteristic threading of our way through messed-up apartments. You and I must have an uncharacteristic drink some day, Kendall."

Kendall said warmly, "Sure. Like to."

Gregory looked at him quickly. "All is well, balanced, in right order, then? Forgiven?"

Windham said, "What are you two talking about?"

Kendall said to Gregory, "Sure. If I dwelt on it I'd get angry all over again, but common sense tells me now that your attitudes are simply a necessary reflection of your job. Also—"

Windham repeated loudly, "What are you two talking about?"

Kendall said, "Oh, sorry, Major—" and thought that Windham's pomposity must often have caused him to be excluded from conversations.

"We were just commenting that Kendall no longer seems so angry. I told you how he felt when I left him last night."

"Ah—yes. Glad to know you feel better about our, uh, necessary part in your, uh, affairs. Is Miss Wentwirth better?"

"Still sleeping. Breathing evenly. I think she'll come through it all right."

"Good." Windham sounded really pleased. "And your hands?"

"They hurt." Kendall held them out. "And they're damned awkward to manage. But I'll live, too."

Windham repeated, "Good."

He seems to be in a rut, Kendall thought, and then wondered why they were there at all.

Gregory answered the thought. "Well, then, we'll be going. We came really just to see how you felt. The doctor expects you this afternoon. You have the address he left you?" Kendall nodded. "Also thought you might feel better if you knew that we intend to keep men stationed back and front, just in case. Until the—uh—time limit runs out—"

Windham said, "You've forgotten, Gregory, that there is one other thing I wish to say." He chose a chair with deliberation and dropped into it as though he were padded with lead.

Gregory shrugged and perched on the edge of a straight chair, and Kendall returned to the couch.

Windham clasped his hands over his middle and continued: "I understand, Mr. Kendall, that Gregory misled you last evening. It is true that we were fortunate in catching those men. And perhaps the emergency may be a little less acute, but I will certainly not feel safe until I have —uh—apprehended the message I still think is secreted in this—"

Kendall said, "Major—"

But Windham could not be stopped in mid-statement. He held up his hand for attention, frowned slightly, and went on as if the interruption had not occurred—"in this apartment. And I must add that I am certainly in a better position than Mr. Gregory to appreciate the—"

Kendall said loudly, "Major!" This time he succeeded in bringing Windham to an annoyed halt. Kendall lowered his voice and added, "I have found the message."

Gregory's face jerked violently in Kendall's direction, and its subtly amused expression—the result of watching Windham stopped in mid-sentence—was replaced by a look of intense seriousness.

Windham, however, became more expressionless than ever. He said, "Indeed?" Then even he found that insufficient. "Have you it here? Of course you have it here. May I have it? Please? I mean—" He stopped.

His disjointedness had a sobering effect on Kendall. He rose and walked over to the desk, and as he picked up the little slip the full meaning of the message came home to him. He had understood it—in the sense that it made sentences in English for him. But its implications had not really seeped through to him until that second.

He handed the slip of paper to the major, who studied it briefly and then raised his eyes to Kendall's. Of course, Kendall thought confusedly, if you knew the meaning in advance the words would translate for you quickly and easily.

Windham said, and his voice seemed to come with difficulty, "But you didn't make anything of this—this mishmash—did you?"

There was a frankly longing note in his voice, and Kendall almost left the matter there. But it wouldn't do—not for a number of reasons, of which simple honesty was not the least. He said slowly, "Yes, Major, I'm afraid I did. The words, and most of the meaning."

Windham said, "I see."

There was silence in the room.

Then Gregory stood up. "Well," he said briskly. "I must be going. Things to do. I'll leave you two together. You'll excuse me, Major?" It was an empty politeness. He was obviously sure he would not only be excused, but was not wanted. "Kendall—"

"I'll walk you to the door."

As they left the living room, Kendall had the uncomfortable feeling that the major hated to permit him out of his sight.

At the door, Kendall asked in a low voice, which he

hoped would be excused on the grounds that Marta was not to be disturbed, "Am I in for it?"

"I'm afraid so. Not your fault, of course. Actually, we're extremely grateful. But the major wanted it both ways: he wanted you to be bright enough to find the thing, and dumb enough not to understand it. When you and I get together, by the way, I'd like to know how and where you found it—if that's not violating the restrictions that are about to be wrapped around you like steel laths."

"Sure. Be glad to explain. It's pretty simple."

The door had started to close and Kendall had turned back toward the living room when Gregory said, "Oh, and Kendall—"

"Yes?"

"I wish you great happiness." The door closed.

XXIII

Kendall said, "I'm sorry, Major. There is nothing to be done about it. Can you take my word for the fact that I shall never divulge a single word of what I read on that slip to a living soul?"

Windham didn't answer the question directly. Instead he asked, "I would like to be entirely certain that you do understand it before I give the consequences any thought. What does it mean to you?"

"Well, exactly what it says. All you have to do is read it downward. Some of it isn't completely clear to me. Those Chinese names I shall have to—" He paused. "I must admit that I shall rush to the nearest atlas and look them up."

Windham half-smiled. Kendall realized he had never seen Windham come even that near a smile before. Windham said, "I'm glad of the admission. At least it gives me a measure of your honesty. But you understand the rest of it?"

"Yes."

"Will you please quote it to me?"

"Well, if you read it fast—which I failed to do at first—it falls into sentences. 'American Chinese will infiltrate. Chemulpo—Weihaiwei. Taitogai—Huithow—'" Kendall hesitated. "I don't know what the 'Pt.' stands for—presumably 'point' or 'port.' Those must be Chinese or

Korean coastal towns. Then, 'Indoctrination Seuta-conawa.' And the rest of it says that the indoctrinated Chinese-Americans, approximately two thousand strong, will land at the ports on March fourth."

"Yes." Windham heaved a sigh. Kendall found himself hoping the major wouldn't cry.

But, unexpectedly, Windham turned businesslike and comparatively cheerful. "It's 'Point.' You're quite correct in your interpretation. Hollister added a little cloudiness to the message by using a couple of old names. It's as if he had called Seoul 'Kaijo'—a name no longer popularly used. But, to hold to his names, Chemulpo, usually called Inchon, is in Korea, just west of Seoul, and just across the Yellow Sea from the China mainland. Taitogai is on the east coast of Formosa, again across from the China mainland. In this instance one crosses the Taiwan Strait to reach the mainland.

"Hollister was very clever and completely single-minded. Your article, which I thought excellent on the whole, had, nevertheless, an undertone of mystery, as if you and your readers were faced by a complicated man whose depths could never be entirely fathomed. But actually, you see, he was very simple. All you have to understand is that he was singleminded. Singlemindedness is a rare characteristic and much misunderstood. Or, at least, not recognized."

The major paused and then added in a strangely humble way, "Please don't think I'm setting myself up as an interpreter of human character, but, you see—" He fumbled and then said, "You see, we have much in common, Hollister and I. I, too, am singleminded."

For all the mental images Kendall had had of Windham with a meek wife and Windham with a sleek mistress, he suddenly knew beyond doubt that Windham had neither. He was joined—firmly, solely—to the United States Army. In his one word—"singlemindedness"—lay the whole measure of Major Windham. And, out of Kendall's newfound participation in the world, came the thought, A true fact and a lonesome one.

Windham said briskly, "So, as I say—the ports are across from each other: the first mentioned in Western control under the understandings of the Armistice; the second in each case on the China mainland."

Kendall had expected the major to be closemouthed and mysterious, and he was consequently mystified by Windham's open explanations. Still, there it was, and he might as well make the most of it. He asked, "But there's something I don't understand. It doesn't seem— What has the H-Bomb to do with all this?"

Windham permitted himself the little half-smile. "Nothing whatever."

Kendall stared uncomprehendingly at him.

"You don't give up easily, do you, Mr. Kendall? Presumably that quality of persistence led you to, uh, gain entrance to this apartment in the first place and then to solve this little code." He tapped the strip of paper he still held. "And now you are determined to cling to your H-Bomb theory. Well, let me tell you that Seutaconawa has had nothing to do with a mechanical explosive, and it never did have. That is a rumor we carefully leaked, and then we rushed in and clamped down on it. Those—ah—*unusually* realistic tactics paid off very well. As we fully understood in advance, we were never able to disabuse some people of the planted misconception, and those are the people who would have been overly curious in any event and would have probed and messed in where they weren't wanted. This way we fed them pap, and they digested it nicely.

"Seutaconawa, Mr. Kendall, is a training ground, a vast camp at which we have been training men. We call the project that is being prepared there 'Operation Boomerang.'

"Briefly, Operation Boomerang consists of the training of a large group of carefully screened American volunteers to do a specific, highly unusual job. Outside of the care exercised in selecting them, these men are just like the servicemen at any other field, except for one thing—they are all of Chinese descent. Their training at Seutaconawa consists largely of a re-education in the knowledge of the present-day land of their forefathers—Chinese traits, dialects, arms, propaganda. Chinese villages, Chinese terrain. Chinese habits, and their current state of mind. Chinese—Well, everything." He paused, then added slowly, "And they are to be let loose on the Chinese mainland."

Kendall repeated slowly, "Operation Boomerang. That's a masterly choice of a name. We are returning them in a real boomerang gesture."

Windham nodded. "That's one interpretation of the operation's title. There are many. Another is the boomerang of infiltration. Infiltration is, after all is said and done, *their* weapon. And still another interpretation is based on the fact that we are using the weapon of propaganda. They have used it to the hilt; we have used it little and not as effectively. Here we shall strike—boomerang—with propaganda, and our propaganda will be the strongest kind of all—truth. This is our answer, finally, to 'agrarian reform.' Someone—an, uh, very important man—saw this as a simple but powerful solution, and because he was so—so high up—he had the power to act on it.

"I'm not going to tell you how these men are trained or how many of them there are—incidentally, that two thousand figure is incorrect—but I will tell you that their weapons, psychological, physical, and—uh—others—are incredibly ingenious." A complacent little sound, like a chuckle, came out of him, and he added, "Quite worthy of the Chinese, in fact."

Kendall realized that the major had made a little joke, and he reached through his fascinated preoccupation to bring up a show of appreciation. "Chinese ingenuity," was all he could manage, "very good." Then he said forcibly, "But it *is* good! The whole plan is magnificent and audacious. It might just work."

"If you knew the details, Mr. Kendall, you wouldn't have a single doubt of its efficacy. The cliché about ingenuity may be applied to the Chinese, but the Americans are the ones who have really earned the right to that adjective. *We* are the most ingenious people on earth; look at our inventions; look at our homes. The plan is infinitely detailed and ingenious. It will stop the Communists—at least in that one area, and it's a vast area. And as the Chinese learn and change their viewpoint—and they will, Mr. Kendall—there is an excellent chance that the whole Orient will be swept along on a tide of honesty. And we will have taken a first step that we will then take again and again—with greater and greater know-how, with more sureness and quicker success.

"Do you know anything about 'brain-washing,' Mr. Kendall?"

"A little. The meaning and origin of the term. Something of the way it is developed and—enforced."

"Well, it's a virulent, insidious poison, and it has been fed to the Chinese, unremittingly, for years. They are thoroughly poisoned. Perhaps time would erase its effects and bring a return to healthful sanity. But—only perhaps. And we can't wait because meanwhile we must fight its results—in one land or another—and in the fighting we lose the youth of democratic lands and we kill off those poor dupes, too. But we don't cure the ones we don't kill. So without an antidote, the slaughter would go on and on, in one country after another, frighteningly, ceaselessly, fruitlessly—

"But this infiltration method, carefully carried out, intelligently expanded, can be the antidote, the antibrain-washing potion—"

In an effort to assimilate the possibilities of the plan,

Kendall withdrew his full attention from Windham, and so it was a minute before Windham's final words echoed back at him. He looked up, startled, and said, "I beg your pardon?"

"I said that as a result of these—revelations—you will certainly understand that I cannot let you go."

"'Let me go'?" Kendall stared at him. "You don't *have* me. Must I remind you again, Major, that you are not a one-man army? Or a secret police? I cannot be held without reason, by you or anyone else! I will give you my word, a solemn pledge of secrecy, that—"

"Mr. Kendall, wait. I am not a very tactful man"—humility in Windham had the force of the vastly unexpected. Kendall found his words dying on his lips—"and I phrased it incorrectly, perhaps. Much of what you say is true. Holding you will be somewhat difficult. But we managed Seutaconawa, Mr. Kendall."

It struck Kendall as being a powerfully persuasive statement.

"We will manage to hold you, Mr. Kendall. And not because I personally wouldn't be willing to accept your pledge, but because no one could make a complete pledge. You might talk in your sleep, Mr. Kendall. You might go suddenly insane. Or suppose they kidnaped you? Can you pledge yourself not to talk under torture, the refinements of which neither you nor I can even foretell?"

No, Kendall thought numbly, I can't.

"We will hold you, Mr. Kendall." The singlemindedness was frighteningly apparent. "But it would be pleasanter and simpler if you would simply give yourself into protective custody."

"For how long?"

Windham looked hopeful. "For about a month. About —uh—thirty-five days. We would make you very comfortable. And we could help you with some information toward articles. Not top-ranking secrets, of course, but many things that have never been published."

Kendall found himself smiling. The offer had been made so earnestly, and with such naïveté. He felt like a child promised candy if he'd go quietly to bed.

Windham seized on the smile. "All right, Mr. Kendall?"

A girl's voice, drowsy and low, called, "Bob. Bob?"

Kendall stood up and said hurriedly, "All right, Major Windham—on one condition."

The major raised his eyebrows.

"That you give me some time, right now—alone—with Miss Wentwirth. In which to explain and, er, plan." He stood up. "And you'd have to take my word of honor for my discretion during that time."

The pause was infinitesimal. Then the major settled back comfortably in his chair. He said, "I have complete faith in your discretion, Mr. Kendall. I'll just sit here."

As Kendall crossed the tiled hall, walking firmly now, all things were in his grasp. Immediately behind him was the major's trust—infinitely worth the having. Immediately before him was Marta.

He opened the bedroom door.